ETCHED IN STONE

Khargals of Duras

ABIGAIL MYST

INTRODUCTION

A thousand years ago, a Khargal scouting party left Duras, only to crash on a planet called Earth.

Injured and outnumbered, the stranded Khargals hid among stone effigies and observed the slow evolution of the planet's primitive inhabitants. With no means of returning to Duras, they watched from their shadowy perches and faded into legend, becoming the mythical gargoyles.

Until today. Long after any hope for rescue had died, the distress signal has finally been answered.

It's time to go home.

ETCHED IN STONE

Frelinray knows duty. He's been protecting the same family for over 80 years. Now the call home has finally arrived. He must choose between serving his people, the Khargals, or the human woman he desires above all others. Which promise should he break?

Jesse has the hots for a stone statue. Ridiculous, but true. She is an artist, and he's her muse, but a girl has to draw a line somewhere. Or so she thinks, until he swoops in to rescue her. Can a relationship between a girl and a gargoyle really work, especially when forces beyond their control are finally calling him home?

PROLOGUE

FRELINRAY

Felinray never thought he'd be glad of the Nazis. They were usually on his list of the worst of the worst. Slimy, racist bastards who would rather shoot something than actually solve the problems in their own lives.

But now, as they dropped bombs by the plane load, he was almost grateful. The men that held Frelinray and his closest friend Tas were either too cheap or too stupid to invest in proper bomb shelters. Perhaps they just thought their prizes were not worth the price of carting deep down into the ground. Either that, or too dangerous. But he was not about to look a gift horse in the mouth, as the human expression went.

They'd been taken, nearly six months before when Tas had insisted on attending that grakking weekly concert. Even with their hats and overcoats, they had been easily distinguishable from the crowd for someone who had been trained in recognizing a Khargyl. There was only so much you could do to disguise horns and a tail.

"Come on, Tas," he said, pulling at the chains that had

secured him to the wall. That wall was no longer intact. In fact, it had fallen down and conveniently left a hole just big enough for him to squeeze through.

"You go," Tas said through the dust. Both of them hunkered down as another shell whistled by and hit a nearby building.

"We've been through this before. I'm not leaving without you."

"Yeah, and we've been through this before. You've got rocks for brains." Tas coughed and some of the dust settled. Felinray got a better view of the damage. Yes, half the wall was down, but only his half. Tas's chains were still firmly imbedded in the wall that was still standing. Felinray now cursed the Nazis and their shoddy aim. He scrambled over the debris to see what he could do. Grabbing a hold on the ancient iron chains that bound them, he yanked. His came away from the wall with ease, free except for the three foot length of chain. He gave a yank on Tas's chain. It held steady in the wall.

"Leave me," Tas said.

Felinray gave the chain another hard pull. Dust and gravel flew as it lifted off the ground.

"I'm sure another few of those bombs will let it loose. It's almost coming now," Felinray replied.

Felinray tugged again, bracing his feet and taking a deep breath, trying to center himself in all the chaos around him. He had to free Tas before the bombing stopped. Otherwise, The Rose Syndicate would come back and they'd both be caught. There'd probably never be another chance like this again.

If Rose came out from their own shelter deep beneath the building to find their two prisoners had nearly escaped, they would never make the same mistake again. It was a rare window of opportunity and Frelinray was determined to use it. He pulled harder on the chain. The wall made an eerie moan and he was encouraged.

"Frelinray, cease. This is futile. Listen. The bombs are stopping. It's too late for me."

"No. I will not leave you!"

"Open your eyes, stupid."

Tas unfolded his wing. It was clearly snapped along the joint. He grimaced in pain. "I'd hit the river and sink like a rock."

Frelinray's heart sank as he digested the truth. They were in some warehouse-type building close to the Thames, that much they had figured out by the sounds of water traffic and the smell of fish. It would take a leap off the building and a glide across the river to escape. With a broken wing, they'd have to go along the streets where they were vulnerable to the thousands of spooked Londoners who were emerging from the shelters.

"I can't," Felinray said defeated. "I won't."

"Look. You have someone. You have your pretty female waiting for you. I have nothing. Nothing at all but my broken self. Go. Besides, I know you well enough to know you'll come rescue me." He grinned a toothy smile and took a deep breath. "Go," Tas repeated.

The noise of footsteps sounded below them. Their captors were coming out of the shelter and investigating. Soon, it would be too late.

"I'll hold them back. Go," Tas said.

Finally, Frelinrey nodded. He grasped the hand of his friend, his brother, and then scrambled over the rubble toward the open spot in the wall. He pulled himself up as he looked over the edge. Sure enough, they were in the third story of a building right on the waterfront. Frelinray grabbed the chains that trailed from the manacles on his wrist. He spread his wings wide and took a leap.

There was that thrill of being suspended in air, wings stretched and open, catching the wind. With the chains weighing him down, it was only a strong draft that kept him aloft. He knew that he could not have carried Tas with his own chains and still kept the two of them above water.

He noted the buildings, but it was dark, black out dark and there was little moonlight to assist him. The only light came from the fires that raged from the newly gutted buildings. Frelinray could see better than his human counterparts in the dark, but he hardly recognized the London he'd known maybe six months earlier. He had to guess at the time that had passed, as he'd been kept in a box for a large portion of his capture.

So much of London lay in rubble that it was hard to get his bearing. He opened his wings and gave one last push up to the top of a short building on the other side of the river. He had made it that far, but he had to push further. He was still too exposed, too noticeable and Rose had eyes and ears everywhere. It was best to find some old church and hide among the gravestones, preferably far from London and its Nazi bombs. But only after he found Jessenia. Only once he knew that she was safe from harm could he rest in stony silence.

She lived nearly a mile from here, but with luck, he could hop from one rooftop to another unnoticed. The damn chains were nuisance. He couldn't just let them hang, but carrying them wasn't optimal either. They didn't leave his hands free and threw off his balance, even using his tail as a counterweight.

Frelinray turned toward Jessenia's flat and scouted his route ahead. The sound blast from behind him nearly knocked him over and the flash of light blinded him for a long moment.

When he could see again, he turned and squinted at the source of the explosion.

The building he had just flown from across the river, was a smoldering shell. Rose must have been storing explosives alongside them in the warehouse. With the searing heat on his skin and the acrid smoke and crackle, it was more than just a Nazi bomb that had leveled the building. Men scrambled out of hiding and began to man the water cannons to stop the damage from spreading. He dare not go back to look.

Even in durammna, the stone sleep of his kind, a Kargyl

would have been blown apart by the force of such an explosion. Tas, his friend, his brother, was dead. There would be time for mourning, centuries even, but now he had no time.

"Goodbye, old friend."

Frelinray gathered his chains once more and leaped to the next rooftop and then to the next, spreading his wings to glide across each span. Most were narrow, especially further away from the river. Many of them were half crumbled from a previous blitz, but he was able to make good time. It was near to daybreak when he finally reached the little cramped flat where he and Jessenia had fallen in love.

She was too young for him, too young, too fragile, but all humans were, when it came to that. He was nearly two thousand Earth years old and yet, when she spoke to him, when she laughed, all he could think of was wanting to spend the rest of his days with her. And that was his plan, to take her away from the war, from the fighting. Some place quiet where the two of them could raise a family and he could let time continue on. He was ready for that now. More than he had ever been in the thousand or so years he'd spent marooned on this backward planet. He knew others of his race had found a match and had settled down, choosing to let their lives play out, but he had always thought they were crazy. Better to stay a stone and wait for rescue than to waste away your existence on this puny little rock.

But then he had met Jessenia. And all his doubts had melted away. They were never going to get rescued. The sigil would never shine. So he would make the best of it here. Have a few sons and make a real life with her.

Frelinray had no illusion that Jessenia would leave her two younger sisters and come away with him alone. Olivia was a precocious child that had grown up too fast, only sixteen, while Margaret was just ten years old. Their mother had died five years ago. All three sisters lived together in the small flat with their father, at least until he had shipped out to France and left Jessenia to take care of her younger sisters.

Frelinray had long accepted that he would have a ready-made family and his children would grow up alongside their aunts as one large family unit. He had money. Lots of it. He could buy an estate out in the country and they could live there together in peace and harmony. Finding a husband for Olivia would be a daunting task, but with the proper dowry (and the right amount of frighteningly mysterious father-figure), he was sure he could get the job done.

He breathed a sigh of relief when he saw that their building and the two surrounding it were intact. One building a few down had caved in, but it must have been a few weeks ago, as the rubble had already been managed and the Londoners had routed around it like a colony of stubborn ants.

They had that trait in common. He landed on the roof, tired and ready to stone sleep, but he would be uneasy until he found Jessenia, until he wrapped his arms and wings around her and felt her lips on his. The light came over the edge of the buildings and Frelinray tried the door. She had always left it unlocked for him, but this morning, it was locked shut, bolted from the inside. He probably had enough strength left to tear the thing off its hinges but that in itself would have been a bad way to announce himself after six months of unexplainable absence.

He knocked, and then sat back on his haunches, and waited. Minutes ticked by and without really meaning to, Frelinray found himself edging toward his old habit, stone sleep. The sun began to warm his hardened skin and the relief of being free sunk into his bones. He nearly entered the second phase when the door opened. Olivia peered around the edge of it.

She gave him a funny look, eyeing him from head to toe, and then closed the door back behind her.

Twenty minutes later, Olivia returned, lugging the largest pair of bolt cutters he'd ever seen.

"Think this will get the job done?" she said, gesturing towards his chains. Trust Olivia to be practical before even putting in the niceties. She put the bolt cutters up against one of the chain links and put all her weight into closing them but they didn't budge. If he weren't so anxious to get rid of them, he might have been amused.

He took the cutters from her, and using the ground as a pivot point, he shoved them in the manacle lock, forcing it down with all the strength he could muster. It snapped with a loud clang and one hand was free. He quickly repeated the process for his other wrist and then threw down the chains with a sigh of relief examining the wrists he hadn't seen for six months.

Olivia tried to pick up the chain. "How am I supposed to explain this to the scrappers? I was using it to hold my gorilla? But then the damn Nazis got him?"

Frelinray didn't especially like being compared to a primate, but he was in no mood to take exception.

"Where is Jessenia?" he inquired.

"I haven't even had my tea yet. You're welcome, by the way," Olivia replied, evading his question.

"Hello, Olivia. Nice to see you. Where is your sister?" Frelinray repeated.

"They sent Midge off to some farm in the country. She's at least trying to take all in stride, pretending she's some famous explorer off to the wilds of Africa."

"Not that sister," Frelinray said, impatiently.

"I know. We got news, by the way. Daddy didn't make it. Dunkirk. Got almost across the Channel." She turned and sighed, staring at the ground. "At least we got a body." As if that was some solace for losing her only parent.

"I'm sorry," he told her.

"It's alright. Everyone leaves. Or dies. Or leaves and then dies. Honestly, you're the first one to come back."

"It wasn't my fault. I was captured, held prisoner. I wouldn't have left Jessennia, you girls," he said as he motioned to the chains. "But I got free. And I promise, we'll all go, the four of us, to where it's safe."

"Four?" There was something in her voice that made his skin crawl ominously. She was stalling, waiting, and in his heart, he knew, deep down that something was terribly wrong. He almost didn't have the breath to ask.

"Olivia. What happened?"

"She went looking for you. Every afternoon, the church-yards, the buildings, anywhere she could think to find a big statue or thing like you. She kept saying, you'd never just leave on purpose, without saying anything," Olivia stammered, beginning to tear up.

"I wouldn't. They took me," he remind her.

"I know. I even joked about it. That you'd gone secretly away to Germany, to kill Hitler and get this nonsense over with quickly so that Daddy would let you... though that was never going to happen. I mean, you've got wings! Definitely not normal."

"Olivia."

"They say she got caught in a raid. Two weeks ago. She's gone. It's just me here now. I lied. Told them I was eighteen in order to stay here with her. But now, it's just me."

He collapsed onto the rooftop, wanted to crumble into a million pieces. Wanted go into a deep stone sleep and not emerge until the wind had worn away his features to nothing.

"Please," he heard Olivia cry. Her tears had truly erupted now. She'd probably not allowed herself to mourn either her sister or her father properly. "Please don't leave me alone."

He held out his arms and she stepped into his embrace. He folded his wings around them. It was not the embrace of love that he had longed for, that his bones ached for, but one of protection. He would not abandon Olivia.

❧ I ☙

JESSE

The bathroom was trying to kill her. At first, it had been a simple toilet banshee, a high pitched whine in the old pipes every time she flushed the toilet. Then, an entire chunk of tile had crashed down near her toes while she had been showering. With just enough of a rinse to get the shampoo out of her hair, Jesse hopped out around the debris and toweled off. She grabbed the nearest clothing, a ratty t-shirt she normally painted in, and an equally spotted pair of jeans.

"Crap, crap, crappity, crap!" she sang to herself.

She was going to have to see the super. She hated going to see the super. For a start, he was old and grumpy. Secondly, and most importantly, every time she went to see him, she expected him to remember that she owed him money. A lot of money. She scraped up rent when she could, but for the past two years of occupying her studio apartment, she'd missed quite a number of months.

The life of an artist wasn't easy in New York. She still

couldn't quite see how her Aunt Olivia had managed it for all those years. Probably the same way she had: hoping and praying that the super, Ray, would keep forgetting about the rent.

Jesse missed Olivia. She had been the youngest old person Jesse had met when she'd been dropped off that first summer when she'd been ten. Right away, Jesse had been put to work, holding iron bars while her great aunt welded them in some pattern that only she could see.

That's where she'd caught the bug. Art. It had seeped into her veins and into her heart. Working a desk job would have probably killed her.

If the tile didn't get her first.

Jesse had never understood why the building owner let the super live in one of the two penthouse apartments. She would have thought that it would have been the highest rent in the building and therefore premium, but no, Jesse shared that luxury with not a hot, rich celebrity but a grumpy old man that she rarely saw unless she was actively seeking him out. Most of the time, it felt like she had the space to herself.

Her studio was actually two levels, a living level with her twin bed, kitchen and couch, and her art level, up a narrow set of stairs that opened up to a grand set of skylights. Her apartment opened up to a rooftop garden that she knew Ray must totter around in because it was always watered and pruned. There was enough space for her to take her art outside and paint when the weather was good.

There was a large gargoyle statue in the corner that stooped over the street as if watching and waiting to swoop down upon some unsuspecting person below. It had been there for as long as she could remember.She remembered asking Olivia about it on several occasions, but her aunt had been cagey about its origins. The sculpture didn't seem to jive with Olivia's usual aesthetic. Usually, she was in to randomly placed arms and rather abstract statuary. But this was a well sculpted, proportionate male gargoyle that could only be described as handsome.

As a child, he had fascinated her. She'd always imagined that he had his own story. She'd talked to him, even though she'd never given him a name, and stroked the smooth stone of his wing. As a teenager, she'd ogled over his perfectly chiseled chest and his prominent chin. The bones beneath his eyebrows curled out just enough to settle into two small horn points on his head, which Jesse thought made him look more mischievous than devilish, though the frown on his face was sad and heart heavy.

Sometimes, she even fancied that he moved.

Jesse didn't take the garden entrance to Ray's apartment. That would have been a little creepy. She respected his privacy and he respected hers. Instead, she took the hallway past the elevator that led to his front door. She rang the bell and waited. Nothing. She was beginning to suspect that Ray was hard of hearing.

"Ray?" She knocked again. Something banged in his apartment. Good. That meant he was home (not that she ever saw him leave) and he was awake. She hoped that she hadn't woken him up. It was nearly nine in the morning and surely that was a respectable time to knock on someone's door. Oh, God, she hoped he didn't sleep in the nude. Great. Now the image of Ray's wrinkly old backside was running through her brain.

The door swung open and there was Ray, fully dressed as he normally was, in a button down shirt, sweater, and a pair of khaki slacks. He had a brown fedora on his head. Jesse could swear he probably showered with it, because she'd never seen him without it.

He said nothing. Just stared at her in a silent broody manner, as if he were thinking of something totally else while he stared at the wall behind her.

"Hi, Ray. My ceiling just came down on me. I was nearly knocked out by a tile in my shower," Jesse said as she pointed back toward her apartment.

"Tile."

"Yes. On my head. And while you're at it, the toilet banshee is getting louder."

"What's a toilet banshee?"

"There's a loud screeching noise every time I flush. Can you fix it?"

"Toilet. Tile."

"Yes. Do you want to come and see?"

Ray stood there for a moment, as if he hadn't heard the request.

"I should."

"Yes. You should."

Jesse felt bad about bothering the man, but she wasn't about to let that kind of thing go. Once the tile started falling, it meant more was probably on its way. She turned, and headed back to her apartment. Ray followed. How could such an old man walk so heavily? He sounded like a linebacker as he headed down the hall behind her.

Jesse entered her apartment and Ray stopped to look around. Despite her aunt's death being nearly 18 months ago, Jesse had changed very little. It was as if she were still living here for the summer. Any minute her aunt would come around the corner fresh with some crazy new art piece in her brain. It was a happy ghost of a memory that she lived with. Jesse couldn't have been more thrilled than when Olivia's lawyer had told her that the entire studio and its contents had been willed to her.

She shouldn't have been surprised. She was Olivia's only living heir. Most of her family had died during World War Two. Only Olivia and her sister Margaret had immigrated to New York. Margaret was Jesse's grandmother who had died when Jesse was two. Her own mother had raised Jesse on her own after her father split.

As a single mom, she'd only too happy to send her kid off to Olivia for the summers for some free day care. Then Jesse's mom had gotten sick and had gone quickly. From diagnosis to death in six months. She'd said it was a blessing. "Some people linger for years," her mom had said, but still didn't stop Jesse from crying over it all, and feeling a load of self pity at being an orphan in the world.

"Plenty of people are orphans," Olivia said. "You have to make your own family, no matter how strange they are."

Jesse had a sneaking suspicion that she'd somehow been talking about Ray, even though she was pretty sure they weren't lovers. In fact, she'd never seen her aunt with anyone, male or female. Besides, Olivia had been near 90 when she'd passed. Ray couldn't possibly be that old, though he had been old as long as she could remember.

How did someone politely ask an old man his age without offending him?

Jesse led him into the bathroom, though she was sure that his apartment was a mirror of hers. He followed her in and stood in the doorway. She pulled back the shower curtain and pointed up. Sure enough, another chunk of tile had come down while she'd been gone. There were now three large chunks in the bathtub.

"Yup. It's coming down," rumbled Ray.

"Can you fix it?"

"I told Olivia the whole thing should have been gutted years ago."

"Why didn't you?"

"Because she didn't want it. It was a pain just to get her to let me put in the grab bars."

Jesse eyed the bars next to the toilet and the tub. There were definitely the newest fixtures in the place.

"You offered to get the place redone?"

"Yup."

"You offering now?"

"Yup."

"What kind of renovation are we talking about?"

"You're the artist. Draw me a picture." With that, Ray turned and left the bathroom. "Until then you can use my shower. Back door's always unlocked."

With that, Ray left and closed the door behind him.

"Well."

✣ 2 ✣

FRELINRAY

This was never going to work. Not in a million years. Frelinray swooped out to the garden, took his normal spot, and let his body relax into a stone sleep. He did not slip into a deep sleep. He needed to think.

She was the image of her great aunt. She even shared her name, Jessenia. Every time he saw her, he froze, somehow expecting to flash that same smile, that knowing glance, to reach out with her finger and trace the ridges of his brow to the point on the top of his head. It was the main feature, besides his wings that marked him as an alien to this world. Even now, after eighteen month of seeing Jesse, watching her, caring for her, Ray, as she called him, could not stop that gut reaction.

As a child, she had stroked his wings, and he had found comfort in it. When she did it now, he felt like breaking his sleep and howling out his desire for her.

But this wasn't his Jessenia. This was Jesse. Nonetheless, he'd promised Olivia, just as he'd promised her so many years before. The worlds still echoed in his head.

"She's all that I have left, Ray," Olivia had said, only days away from her impending death.

15

"I know. But it has to be her choice." Her grandmother, Margaret, had fled from his care as fast as she could, got married young, died young. She'd been a blink on the surface of the world. Olivia had weathered the ages.

"She's more like me than Midge. She'll get you."

"You haven't told her yet?"

"No. I haven't quite found the words for..." Olivia turned away at that moment, lost for the right phrase.

Ray supplied it. "My almost-brother-in-law is a gargoyle space alien and he's going to watch over you when I croak?"

"You see my point?"

"Then put it in a letter," he suggested.

"She's going to think her dear old Aunt Olivia went bonkers in the end."

"Her dear old Aunt Olivia has gone bonkers if she thinks me telling her is going to work any better."

Olivia smiled and nodded, waving him away.

"Fine, fine. I'll write a letter," she conceded.

Olivia had died in her sleep three days later. She still hadn't written the letter.

There were so many things Ray had not explained to Jesse. Every time he saw her, his mind flashed back to her great aunt, the love of his life, and his words were stolen from him.

Ray kept telling himself there was time and plenty of it. Jesse didn't seem to be in a hurry to go anywhere, though he found it troubling that she hadn't really changed anything from when Olivia had lived there. Surely a twenty-something would want some changes in living spaces from a ninety year old. He'd waited for a request, but Jesse had just moved in and started to create art, as if she were her aunt.

The biggest difference he could see was that Jesse had no friends, no visitors. She spent much of her time alone and no one had come to the apartment that he had noticed. Olivia had not been shy around bringing people round. Men or women.

Ray told himself not to pry, but his old instincts were kicking in. It wasn't healthy to spend so much time alone. He should know. He'd spent several centuries that way. That was the way of his people. They were nothing if not patient.

He'd wait a few more days until she came looking for him again. Then, maybe he could get over the way her dark hair fell on her shoulders, just as her namesake. The way the same eyes that haunted his dreams stared back at him without the slightest hint of recognition. He didn't blame Jesse for not wanting to get to know an ugly old man in an outdated sweater. Perhaps, if he could fix his blasted perception filter, things would be easier.

He waited until dark, until the lights had been off in Jesse's studio for a good hour, then shook off the stone sleep and headed into his apartment. He opened his workbench and pulled out the tools that he'd cobbled together in the last century. It was like working with sticks and rocks compared to the technology of his kind. They'd achieved space travel before Earth had discovered fire. Ray had to admit that they'd been picking up the pace in the past fifty years, and trying to repair and replace bits of his tech by using Earth tech had become something of a hobby of his lately.

Olivia had laughed the first time he'd managed to program the perception filter. She'd insisted on an outfit that would let him blend right in so he'd chosen an unassuming older man. She begged him to go on a walk in Central Park in broad daylight so they went. They'd even fed the pigeons. Then the circuits had fused and it had gotten stuck. He'd be a funky old man until he got off this rock.

Every once in a while, he ordered some intriguing new tech and took it apart, seeing if there was anything that he could use or tinker with to fix his perception filter, or to add to his designs. At one point or another, he'd designed all the major components of a ship that could get him back up into space and off this planet. Building the thing wouldn't be all that difficult either.

Opening a wormhole that would get him close enough to home was the real issue. While he had a knack for space design and engineering, his knowledge of spatial mechanics and astrophysics were still basic level. He didn't have a way to generate enough power to tear a hole in the universe by brute force and he didn't have the skill to direct it where he wanted to go.

So it was either stay here and wait for rescue or take the long way home. And there was no guarantee that wouldn't be another few thousand more years gone. It had already been near a thousand. Who knew? Maybe the war that had torn his world in two had been over for years. He had no way of knowing.

Ray had several packages on his bench waiting since the last time he'd gone on a shopping spree. Amazon was a wonder. No longer did he have to ask Olivia to procure him some random electronic that he'd read about in a magazine. Instead, he managed a few clicks and it arrived on his doorstep in two days, no questions asked.

Ray opened a box with his nail and pulled the device out of its layers of plastic bubbles and paper. It was a newer, supposedly more advanced version of the camera that he'd already gutted for pieces, hoping that some human would have developed just the right system that would be compatible with his perception filter.

He cracked open the case to stare at the guts. No. Apparently, 'new and improved' was more advertising than reality. He put it aside and opened the next box, not entirely optimistic. Something clattered behind him, out near the garden. He swirl around on his stool and scrambled toward the French door that he had left open. He paused in the center of the patio and took stock. Nothing was disturbed or out of place. He eyed the other buildings that surrounded them.

He couldn't see any other lights on, but that didn't mean anything. Someone could have gotten drunk and decided to kick over a bucket on their way back in after a smoke break. The weather was still quite nice and all was right with the night. He didn't feel like going in and opening the rest of his packages so he resumed his spot on the ledge and drifted off into a deep stone sleep.

❄ 3 ❄

JESSE

J esse had been drawing bathrooms for the past two days and each one got more and more fanciful. She couldn't get that stupid thought out of her head. What kind of man says "draw a bathroom?"

Her current sketch had a toilet that vaguely resembled some sort of odd tuba and a tub that was sunk into the floor like a mermaid lagoon. The walls were covered in reflective scales. It was as if a five year old with a fish fetish had thrown up all over her notebook.

No. That wouldn't do at all. Jesse carefully pulled the sketch out of the notepad and lay it next to the one that looked like some sort of beauty parlor gone wrong. She was not an interior designer. She should show her designs to that fedora wearing grandpa and get him to pick one. Where he thought the money was coming from to pay for it was anyone's guess. The man seemed to have no clue about finances.

She needed a shower. No, she needed a good long soak in a tub with power jets. Maybe she could convince him to put a jacuzzi on the roof. That would be lovely. He'd probably keep his fedora on while soaking. She giggled and let her pencil run wild

20

over a fresh piece of paper. An inset tub with jets and a fedora-wearing form settled deep in the water. Except it wasn't Ray that she drew. It was the gargoyle. And he looked like he was enjoying himself. As sexy as she had drawn him, hat drawn low over his face with little more than a cheeky grin and a pair of fangs showing, Jesse wouldn't mind joining him in that tub.

Lord knew she was well overdue for any kind of male company, but living in a city like this afforded few opportunities for meeting anyone not interested in a quick hook up. Jesse had had her fill of those. No, she was not in the mindset of the latest swipe app and a quick fix. She had some electronics that took the edge off with a buzz in the right area.

It was her mother's fault, Jesse told herself. After her father took off, there was little else her mother was interested in sharing about men and relationships other than 'you don't need them', and 'don't get pregnant'.

She couldn't get pregnant fantasizing about gargoyles in bathtubs, that was for sure. She turned her attention to the other bathroom features. This gargoyle didn't need a tuba toilet. No, he needed something simple, with clean lines. It should be full of light, but not shiny. Classic rock of ages, smooth and polished.

She finished the drawing and for once, was actually pleased with the design. It was probably a twenty grand renovation, but hey, she wasn't paying for it. Of course, Jesse couldn't show this version to Ray, not with the gargoyle in his fedora. That would just be weird. But she could draw the same sketch and hand it to him without a gargoyle. Though not quite yet. Right now, she really needed a shower, and since hers was out of order, she thought she'd take a deep breath and actually take him up on his offer to use his.

She grabbed a towel and put together a little bucket of toiletries to take with her. Then, she grabbed some shower spray and a couple of rags, just in case. She'd never seen a cleaning crew over there, so there was no telling whether the whole exercise was going to be an experience in gross old man funk. In the year and a half she'd been living in Olivia's place and in all the summers she'd spent there, Jesse had never done so much as peeked into the two French doors that lay at the other end of the courtyard.

They were covered with drapes on the inside, and perhaps, she had been more interested in daydreaming at what lay beyond than actually investigating an old guy's apartment. She had always assumed they were unlocked. Apparently, Ray was unconcerned with security. The only way to get to the garden was to go through one of their apartments, so most people in the building probably had no clue that the space was up there.

Jesse pondered what to wear and finally settled on a pair of pajamas with a full robe on top. No sexpot here. Just a girl trying to get clean. She strode across the garden to the doors, which were, for the first time in her memory, actually open. Perhaps he had been expecting her.

"Hello? Ray? I'm here for a shower!"

She stepped in through the door and could not have been more surprised by the decor. She'd been expecting old man stuck in the 80's clutter, but instead, she saw sparse clean modern lines with updated tech everywhere.

"Ray?" This could not possibly be his apartment. She'd somehow stepped into a portal and been transported to some millionaire's bachelor pad. The kitchen alone was to die for. It had beautiful granite countertops and a bar with several large sturdy chairs. A huge television nearly covered one wall. His bedroom must be up in the loft, because she could not spot a bed anywhere. She totally wanted to check out the fridge, but that would be snooping, and she really needed a shower.

There was something else odd about the layout of the apartment, but Jesse couldn't put her finger on it. She shrugged and headed to the bathroom. There was no toilet banshee in here.

Modern immaculate and spacious. It didn't have a tub, but it did have a gigantic rain shower with all the bells and whistles.

Jesse closed the door behind her and made sure it actually locked. Again, old man walking in on her was not ideal. She shed her robe and pajamas and then played with the different knobs and dials. Even the shower was modern tech infused. There were probably a hundred different settings.

"Why do you need a programmable shower?"

Then she selected one, stepped in and absolutely changed her mind. The water fell around her like warm rain, cascading from her hair and down the tips of her breasts. It cycled through a jet phase and all the tension that had been building up melted away. She totally forgot about the owner of the shower and let her mind drift into the tub with her gargoyle.

FRELINRAY

This. This was not supposed to drive him crazy. This was simply the way things had to be. Jesse in his shower, naked. He had never thought such blatant thoughts could surface with such an innocent situation.

Her shower was just broken, that's all. He was being perfectly right in offering his. That didn't stop certain parts of him turning hard, and it wasn't because he was going into stone sleep.

He needed something to do, something not in his apartment. Maybe her shower wasn't as bad as it had appeared. He entered her apartment and headed straight for the bathroom. He looked up at the ceiling and then down at the tiles that still lay in the tub. Nope. The whole thing needed to be gutted, had probably needed gutting ten years ago when he had redone his. He reached up and ran a hand along the tile, pulling a few more down into the tub. There wasn't really even a way to patch it without redoing the entire ceiling, and he couldn't imagine what raining tile would do to Jesse's sensitive skin.

Damn. He was thinking about skin again. He'd love to sit and watch the rain shower rolling off her soft curves.

But she was not his. Even if she looked like Jessenia, there was no telling how she'd react to seeing his real form, to being in a relationship with an honest to goodness alien.

There were perks to mating with a Khargal as he'd explained to her great aunts when he'd been courting Jessenia, . The exchange of the vows, the bite, would change her on a cellular level. It would allow her to carry his children and extend her life, perhaps even double it. He'd heard stories of mates gaining strength or developing other abilities not common to their class or species.

He'd explained all this to Jessenia, and, according to the custom of the time, he'd agreed to wait until they were married before indulging in that facet of their marriage. The 1940's were quaint like that. Now, women were much more open and liberated about sex before marriage.

Ray was not sure he could manage to make love to Jesse without biting and claiming her as his forever. Again, he was way ahead of himself.

He scooped up an armful of the tile and headed back out to the garden. At least he could make use of some of this situation. Although he'd adapted to human food for most of his dietary needs, the clay in the ceramics would provide a more rounded diet for his needs.

He paused to look at the pile of sketches on her table. Each one was more ridiculous than the next. Surely she couldn't be serious about a unicorn mirror. Then he saw it. She'd drawn a picture of him, in his true form, not Ray the super. And he was in a bathtub, naked and grinning. At least he assumed he was naked except for the fedora.

"What are you doing?" Jesse questioned from the doorway.

He nearly dropped his entire armful of tile.

"Tile."

She looked from the bathroom door to the table where he

was standing. It was not exactly on the way out to the garden, and she knew it.

"Okay, we need to set some ground rules here. A schedule maybe. For both you and me," she said, hands clutching her basket of toiletries in front of her like a shield. That scent was going to linger in his bathroom. It would smell like her. He could not be more relieved that his perception filter would hide his arousal.

"Whatever. Just figured you wanted this tile cleaned up."

"Thanks, but where were you when I knocked?"

He'd been standing right behind her in his stone sleep, but he couldn't tell her that.

"Ms. Maguffin had a garbage disposal issue."

She opened her mouth and then closed it again. He sighed in relief. Hopefully, she wouldn't ask what apartment she lived in, as the mysterious woman didn't exist. He subcontracted out all the other maintenance jobs to a management company. But Olivia had introduced him as the super and so a super he was, collecting her rent (when she paid), and collecting her complaints as they happened. As far as tenants went, she was a pretty easy one to please.

"I like your sketches," Ray said, after standing in silence for a long moment. "I think that one's the most practical." He pointed to the one he starred in.

"Those aren't real suggestions. I was just spitballing. I do that. Just draw whatever comes into my brain. It doesn't mean that I want a bathroom with a tuba toilet."

He cracked a grin. It was probably frightening on an old man face, but she laughed. Finally, a little bit of a connection.

"Gotcha. No musical toilets."

"Actually, your bathroom is spectacular," Jesse said. "Anything close to that would be awesome. Aren't those tiles getting heavy?"

He looked down. They would be heavy for an old man. He

nodded and headed back out to the garden. She didn't follow. She probably was going to get dressed. He looked up and saw the door close and heard the lock click.

So much for having a decent conversation. He piled the tile next to him and took one to taste. He took a bite from the first one and shrugged.

"Needs salt."

He was too lazy to go get some, so he just sat there, staring down at the street below, munching on his snack. A pigeon landed on the ledge beside him.

"Salt, or some nice white wine. Do you think she likes wine? She's an artist. Of course she likes wine. Unless she's a beer kinda girl."

The pigeon seemed unimpressed with this rambling. It seemed more interested in trying to taste one of his tiles.

"Nah, this isn't your style. I swear, I'm not holding out on you."

JESSE

The leaves were brilliant in Central Park this time of year. Last year, everything had been coated with the gloom of mourning her aunt but this year was different. The display of fluttering leaves was a pageant of colors, waiting to be captured in some form or another. And Jesse would capture them all. She'd spent nearly the entire day soaking in the color and taking pictures to preserve as much of it as possible so she could go back to her apartment and recreate a masterpiece that would do this work credit.

It had taken her nearly the entire day to also realize that someone was following her. In fact, she quite suspected that there were actually two of them, working in tandem, like she was some foreign spy that they were keeping an eye on. All of which was ridiculous, because she was a practically starving artist with nothing at all to do worth spying on. Her life was an open book.

Julia Child had apparently been a spy, but she'd been a chef that traveled and made plenty of connections. Jesse had few friends to her name and no real connections other than a few artists that she got together with few days a month in order to network and drum up business. But she made more money selling her work in online stores than she ever did in person.

Jesse tried to tell herself it was just her imagination, but even after circling the building and then the block, she was certain that the man in the jogging wear and the woman putting money in the parking meter for the third time were just too nonchalant to be doing anything but waiting for her to reappear and go into her building.

What to do? Did one call the police? Did she start causing a commotion? Did she go up and talk to one of them? The last thing she wanted to do was go up to her apartment alone, but she was afraid if she tried calling the police, they'd just disappear, making her the crazy lady in need of a little psychiatric help. She kept walking, past her building once more and into the little bodega on the corner.

"Hey Hen!" Luis called from behind the corner. He was the cousin or some string relation to the owner Eric. He was also an outrageous, yet harmless flirt.

"Hi."

"You need milk? I got milk? I got all the fresh milk."

"Not exactly."

"Of course you want milk. Eric's new guy in charge of ordering may have ordered twice as much as needed. But don't tell Eric that because he doesn't want Eric to know."

"Luis."

"Okay, you got me. I am Eric's new order guy. Do you think I can handle the responsibility?"

"There are two dudes following me and I don't know what to do," Jesse said, wanting to cut to the quick.

"Like stalky? I got some boys with baseball bats. They are really good at discouraging assholes. Worked like a charm when my cousin Glenda-"

"No, like in running gear and little ear mics. Like government agency spies."

And there was that look that said she might be a little bat shit crazy, but he stuck with her a bit longer.

"You watch the drawer, and I go take a look," he told her.

"The guy in the blue hoodie with the headphones, and the blond woman near the parking meter. At least that's where she was the last three times I went around the block."

Luis ducked out from around the counter and headed out. He flipped his own hoodie up and disappeared from the doorway. Five minutes later, all hell broke out on the street. A dog barked, a woman screamed and about five cars began honking at once. Luis came racing back into the store and in record time, his hoodie was off and stashed and he was standing behind the register as if nothing had happened.

A cop sauntered in, looked around. Luis rang up a gallon of milk as if he'd heard nothing.

"Coffee's in the back," he called and the cop flashed a thumbs up.

"You ain't kidding," Luis said calmly as he bagged up the milk. "The price of things today… You want to borrow a lottery ticket? How about a scratcher? I got some nice fun scratchers here."

Jesse slapped a ten on the counter. She'd been trying not to spend money, as she was going to be short for the rent again, but Luis's efforts had to be paid for with something. That at least was worth ten dollars and a jug of milk.

The cop exited, toting two coffee cups, and Luis waved at him calmly. Jesse idly scratched off the two scratchers Luis had put in front of her.

"So, I'm pretty sure that there are three of them out there. Or maybe four. I caused a bit of a ruckus and they all acted smooth as glass. Whatcha get into?" he asked her.

"I have no idea."

"Well, they know where you live. And I don't think they're going away, but they might still be a bit distracted." He handed her another hoodie from under the counter. "Put it on and go in the front real slick like. You got locks on your doors?"

"Two deadbolts."

"Good. Good luck. Hey, you won twenty bucks!"

"Keep it."

"Only if you take the milk. Seriously." Jesse grabbed the bag and slick as she could, popped the hoodie on and up over her hair. Professionals probably wouldn't be fooled but at least she had a chance.

Jesse didn't look up, but from under the edge of her hoodie, she could see there were a growing number of city workers putting cones around a large splatter of blue paint while the cops with their coffee looked on with a rather nonchalant coolness to the whole situation.

She made it into the building and elevator before she dropped her hood. Once out of the elevator, she took three large breaths. The door to her apartment was cracked open. She had half a mind to go get Ray, but then she realized, it was possible it was Ray in her apartment, working on the bathroom. She certainly hadn't told him no, exactly, and if he'd taken advantage of her being out all day, he might have started the demolition work already.

Jesse pulled her phone out of her pocket and dialed in 911. All she had to do was push the button and she'd have an instant line. But then she wouldn't look like an idiot if it was just some guy with plumber's crack taking apart her bathroom.

She opened the door and surveyed the apartment. She could smell fresh coffee percolating and the lights were on. There was a man sitting ever so nicely on her couch, sipping coffee with a proper saucer, even. He was definitely not a plumber.

His hair was blond and slicked back in that creepy, I-might-be-a-Nazi way, and yet, there was something very not Nazi about his movements. He was slow to turn around and when he did, he met her gaze with bright green eyes that said he was slightly annoyed that she was taking so long to join him.

"Darling, sit, sit." His accent was thick, but she couldn't quite place it with so few words. Sit came out sounding like seat.

She took a step in and then paused. He certainly didn't look like he was there to attack her, but he very well could be responsible for those people that had been following her all day. Jesse knew she should be more panicked about a strange man in her apartment, but she couldn't imagine such a well dressed man deigning to do the dirty work of abducting a woman in broad daylight. His actions spoke more of an over-privileged asshole than a street thug. A streak of bravado rose in her. Over-privileged assholes she knew how to deal with.

"You are late," he told her.

"You had me followed," she retorted.

"I am a very distinguished client. I have to make sure that I am hiring quality." Jesse didn't believe that for a moment. She still entered but she didn't close the door behind her.

She walked over to the garden and opened that door too, just to be ready. If she had to make a quick escape, she could run into Ray's place and lock that door behind her.

From the front, the man was no less mysterious. There was a large scar that ran along the side of his neck. He was chubby and filled out his expensive suit. It was a lemony yellow with a pink shirt and a white silk tie and pocket scarf. It was definitely too late in the year to be wearing such a spring palette, but he didn't seem to care.

"I am Pablo." He said it as if that were his only name, like Madonna or Cher. "This is an interesting studio you have here."

"Yes. It's also where I live. Which is why I'm surprised to see you here without knocking."

"Oh, is it? The door was unlocked."

"Unlocked?"

"Yes, but don't you want to know why I am here?

"Frankly I'm more concerned about how much you are freaking me out right now," Jesse said.

"I've decided to make an offer."

Honestly, Jesse couldn't see herself taking any offer that this guy made her. Why he seemed to think otherwise was quite a mystery.

"I don't think I'm interested."

"Oh, I plan to make you an offer you can't refuse. I don't like being turned down. Just ask anyone."

If he hadn't been sitting there in his lemon suit sipping coffee from a teacup, Jesse would have thought that sounded like a mobster from a TV movie. Here, it just made him sound like a wannabe gangster.

"I've attained a crystal. And I want it set. I want it specifically set."

"I'm not a jeweler, Mr.-"

"Pablo."

He handed her a card. Sure enough, on one side of the card was a phone number. On the other, a rose and a fancy font that read only Pablo. This guy was either full of himself or the real deal. Jesse had yet to ferret out which.

"On the table is a box with all the information that you need to create my desired object," he continued. It was a simple white box tied with a red bow. It looked like a present or a gag gift out of a cartoon.

"I'm going to have to say thanks but-"

"No, no, don't decide now. I'll leave the crystal with you for the time being. But I am confident that you will say yes."

"I'm not so sure."

He stood up, brushing imaginary crumbs from himself. "Again, twenty thousand dollars is a lot of money. I'm assured you can put that to good use."

"Pardon?"

"Good afternoon, Ms. Jenkins. I'll show myself out." And

with that, the mystery man disappeared as quickly as he had come.

Jesse took a deep breath and then realized that she was still standing there with a jug of milk. She shook her head and headed toward the fridge.

"Who was that?"

She closed the fridge to see Ray standing in the garden doorway, the one that she had left open as her safety route.

"Just a potential client."

"I don't like him."

"Pardon?" Jesse said for the second time in five minutes.

"That man. He's bad news. You should stay away from him." Ray squinted at the door as if Pablo were hiding and listening in on the other side.

"I don't see how that's any of your business."

"If he's in my building, it's my business. What was he really doing here?"

"Ray. Honestly. It's my apartment and I expect you to respect the bounds of my apartment. He was here as my guest and therefore none of your goddamn business."

The grumpy man paused to stare at her. It was clear that she had crossed some sort of line, and she wasn't sure how that had happened. It was one thing to be civil with your super. It was another to have him leave the door open so a stranger could wander in and then blame her for the whole debacle.

"Right," he answered.

He turned, and then turned again. "But that's not exactly true. Olivia told me, made me promise to watch over you. And I always keep my promises."

"I don't need a babysitter. I do quite well on my own."

"Really? Well? How?"

"I make do."

"You don't have any friends, no love life to speak of, and the only business walking through your door is a pretty darn shady character."

So he had been spying on her. It was all true, but she'd croak before she'd admit it.

"Your life doesn't seem to be one raging party either."

"I can pay the rent."

"I can too. I only missed a-"

"Twelve thousand fifty-two."

No. It couldn't be that much, could it? Jesse took a deep breath and tried to count it out. Living in New York was expensive. She wasn't sure how she'd got that far behind. She was going to have to get a real day job and sit behind a desk for hours. Ray knew how much she owed down to the dollar. She'd taken him for a doddering old man who couldn't keep track of how much she owed, but he knew and overlooked it. That's what kind of man had that sort of a apartment that she'd seen the other day. He was sharp as a tack. She owed him money and he had offered his bathroom.

Her emotions must have been all over her face because Ray's own shoulders slumped and skulked out.

"Forget about it," he said and then closed the garden door behind him.

Twelve thousand. Wait, hadn't she just been offered a box worth twenty grand?

Jesse sat down on the couch and stared at the neat white box all tied up with a red ribbon. It was ominous, but it might be the solution to all of her problems. She untied the ribbon.

In the box was a smaller box with a large blood red crystal. The thing was faceted into an odd shape that Jesse had never quite seen before. It was intriguing and the stone felt warm in her fingers. It wasn't a resin casting or cheap glass cut. It felt like a real gemstone. She had little to no knowledge of actual jewels, but if she had to guess, she'd say that this was worth a chunk of change.

Under the box were a series of photographs of a large amulet. It was a dark metallic disc covered in strange symbols. In the center, was the crystal that she still held in her hand. She could see herself sculpting it and pouring a mold. But why they hadn't just taken a silicone mold of the original or scanned it and used a 3D printer to replicate it?

Either way, It would take her a few days and very little in supplies to make a reasonable copy of this thing. She could do it, but should she? Creepy government men versus the possibility of having to go out and find a desk job.

She knew which of the two was going to win. It was time to go condition some clay.

6

FRELINRAY

Ray had not survived over a thousand years on this planet without being able to recognize that someone was bad news, and there was no question in his mind that the fat little man in the yellow suit was definitely bad news. The only question was how bad.

He was itching to answer that question, but he he had to wait until late evening before heading out to the Evensong. It was half bar, half nightclub, half speakeasy for every freak and fetish loving soul out there. During the day, it was a low key place to grab a sandwich or a pub lunch, but at night, when they turned on the neon and the black light, every type of weirdo came in for a drink. This, of course, meant that Ray fit right in, camouflage or not. He'd been in more than once without it, and everyone had just assumed he was high into the body mods or liked dressing in gargoyle drag every so often. No one would ask questions, so it was the perfect place for someone like Ray's contact, Giles, to set up shop.

He was officially a bartender and was pretty good at actually making some colorful and potent cocktails, but his main specialty was keeping track of the occult underground. He had his pulse on what was going on in the spaces between the cracks. He knew which organizations were active and what the chatter was about. Officially, Evensong and Giles were neutral territory, but Ray got the feeling Giles would keep a secret unless there was an innocent about to be harmed.

When the assholes like the Rose Syndicate crossed the line, Giles and his buddies guided certain parties to them and pulled invisible strings to make their plans go awry. As long as there had been a Rose Syndicate, Ray suspected there had been a counter intelligence group to keep them in check. They had no official name, but it was a friend of a friend of Giles that had helped Ray cross the pond and disappear into the wilds of New York after the war.

Tonight, Giles was sporting a blue Mohawk and a pair of cat-eyed red glasses. Together with his black tank top, full sleeve tattoos, and five earrings, he was rocking a very distinct look.

"Well, look who's here. Mr. Antisocial. I've been wondering where you'd gotten yourself off to," he said to Ray.

"You've got my number," Ray said as he slid onto the bar stool. "I assume you still have thumbs to send a text."

Giles stuck his tongue out and then glanced from side to side, as if to check if there was anyone listening. It was still early, so most of the crowd hadn't arrived yet.

"There's a rumor mill going around," Giles continued, "that someone in your general vicinity got an entire can of blue paint dropped on their head today."

Ray just squinted at Giles. "Did it have anything to do with this guy?" Ray said, pulling out and showing Giles a screen grab from the elevator security camera.

"Pablo. My, my, my. If that guy is Pablo, you're in for more trouble than I thought."

"Who is he?"

"The current rumor is that he's the newly hired Rose gun.

And he doesn't pull punches. Straight out sociopath. I'd give him a wide berth."

"Pablo have a last name?"

"Pablo is just Pablo. That's why he's so dangerous."

People with only one name thought they could get away from anything. They'd spent so much time running and hiding that real legitimate systems hadn't caught them yet. If Pablo didn't have a paper trail, an arrest record, then there was no guaranteeing that he could be stopped and arrested by normal means.

Giles shook his head and pulled out his phone. "Now I got a question for you," he said. "What is this?" He slid his phone over to show a picture of an object Ray knew well.

"That is, well, have you ever seen Star Trek?"

Giles rolled his eyes and gave him a look that said, "duh."

"We call it a sigil. It's a sort of com badge thingy. They don't work anymore. Haven't for a millennia."

"Rose is all abuzz about them. Trying to reverse engineer one."

"Good luck with that. They are relayed by a master beacon, and as far as I know, that's been under the ocean near France for forever." Memories of his life aboard ship seem so distant they were practically a whisper of a dream. His species had a long memory, but even that was stretching thin.

"Just keep an eye on your tail. All signs point to the fact that they are up to something nefarious. And I have grown to like these visits, as rare as they seem to be these days. You need to find another Olivia. The old girl was good for you. Got you out of the house," Giles suggested.

Ray rolled his eyes. He didn't need dating advice from a human young enough to be his great great great grandchild. Besides, he'd already had the one great love of his lifetime, and he perfectly planned to ignore all the signs of a second. It was just his body's way of reacting to how similar Jesse looked compared to her great aunt. Jessenia, too, was a memory that was fast slipping away, being replaced with an image of Jesse in tight jeans and baggy sweaters covered in paint.

"I'll think about it," Ray said.

"We all know that thinking about it means you'll go back to your rooftop and freeze frame yourself until I've grown a few more wrinkles and my hair turns gray."

"How will you know under all that blue dye?"

"Ha!" Giles poured a shot of some clear liquid and took a quick look to see if anyone was watching before tossing it back himself. "We all get old sometime. Even stone weathers."

"Not any time soon. But thanks."

Ray nodded and slapped down a twenty even though he hadn't ordered a drink. It had been worth the confirmation of what his gut had been telling him.

Pedro was not only bad news, but he was also Rose Syndicate, the same organization that had imprisoned him in London for six months. They were like a hydra. Cut off one head and two grew back in its place. They were perhaps even more dangerous now because they were much better at being sneaky. It was only because they'd been sloppy before that he had managed to escape.

The memory of Tas was still vivid. The acrid smell of smoke and explosives still haunted him from the corner of the senses. Ray had left him, abandoned him to save his own skin, and it was that decision that had saved his own life, condemning his friend, his only real connection with others of his kind.

Ray stepped into the hallway and activated his perception filter. He didn't like to do much walking on city streets when they were crowded. He was leery about doing it much at all lately with the advancement of digital photography and street cams. His perception filter might fool the brain, but it did little to fool the camera.

7

JESSE

It was amazing how fast the project came together. For some reason, she had a singular focus and worked straight through the night and late into the morning. Her basic sculpture was done around 5 AM and then she crashed while it rested.

The crystal was fascinating the more she looked at it. She started a painting, just waiting for the molds to set, and got caught up for hours in the blood red facets that seemed to reflect a multitude of purples, greens and blues as well. It was a new picture from every angle that she turned it.

The pictures fascinated her as well. It was clear this object resided in an art collection somewhere. They were shot on white backgrounds in high resolution photos that captured every detail. Someone had spent quite a lot of money cataloging this item.

There was writing on it, but none of her searches seemed to come up with anything similar. Was it an ancient rune or some made up movie language?

She couldn't imagine someone was paying her twenty grand to create a replica of a movie prop. Of course this whole thing could be a sham. It could be that he wasn't going to pony up any of the final payment.

Jesse was willing to take that risk, just to be able to sit there and examine the stone for a day or two. That alone had inspired a painting. Plus, she'd still have the molds to go on. She could pour another crystal out of resin but getting the color of it just right was going to be a challenge. Either way, it was worth the time to have her creative juices sparking something that really set her imagination flying.

It was right at the tail end of her first crash that Ray decided to make another appearance. He knocked this time.

"Thought I'd get some more tile," he said, glancing to the wheelbarrow beside him.

"Come on in." She opened the door, glad that the weather was still holding. She could probably go out onto the patio and paint, but perhaps it was better to keep an eye on him from upstairs. That's where her painting was, anyway. She headed upstairs and he got to work, banging up a storm in the bathroom.

Thankfully, she'd already taken most of her personal items out of the space in preparation for whatever remodel he was planning. By the amount of noise he was making, he was taking more than just the tile down. For such an old guy, he was pretty spry. She'd never have guessed that he was fit or ripped under that sweater, especially since he never seemed to go out and exercise.

Jesse put on her headphones and tuned him out, centering in on the explosion of paint in front of her. It was a continuously morphing blob of fire that was inspired by the jewel. She still didn't have the color right. It needed more blue and purple. But that was going to have to wait.

Her stomach was growling. She looked at her phone and noticed it was nearly 2 PM. No wonder she was hungry. She headed down the stairs and opened the fridge. The offerings were slim except for the gallon of milk.

Cereal it was! She poured herself a bowl of the frosty marshmallow cereal she had stashed away in the back of the cupboard. It was always her hope that she'd forget it was there, but hunger was a great motivator to search high and low and rediscover the things you'd bought on impulse and really should have tossed before.

Ray exited the bathroom, wheeling a barrowful of debris from her shower as if it were light as a feather. It looked as if he had broken up the tub into smaller pieces in order to haul it out. Where he planned to put it all was quite a mystery.

Ray stood there watching her consume some of the cereal in her bowl. He looked over at the counter.

"That's a lot of milk for one person," he said.

"It was on sale."

She wasn't sure if that was a hint or not. Was he trying to get invited in for a glass of milk or a bowl of cereal or was he just being a slightly weird old man trying to make conversation?

"Would you like some?" she offered, grudgingly.

"Sure. Let me move this."

He disappeared out the door with another load so Jesse decided to take a peek at the bathroom.

"Holy cow!"

He had managed to take half of the bathroom down to the studs. How one man had managed that much demolition in an hour was beyond her. Okay, so maybe he was thirsty.

Jesse grabbed a glass out of the cupboard and poured a full glass of milk. Ray came in and she handed it to him. He stood there and put the glass to his lips. The entire situation was odd. Like she'd stepped into an episode of Twilight Zone. Jesse realized that not only was Ray not sweating or flushed from all the labor, there wasn't a spot of dirt on him.

Had he had time to change while wheeling the bathtub out of the room? She imagined that he had an entire wardrobe full of the navy sweaters, but even his hat looked fresh and clean from the start.

She watched him drink the whole glass without stopping. He handed it to her and she filled it up again. He drank the second glass as quickly as the first.

"Thank you. I'll leave the toilet for now. I'm sure you'll want at least that. I can start work on building the new substructure."

"Are you doing all the work yourself?"

He shrugged. "Most of the demolition. I find it cathartic. I'm good at tearing things apart. I've got a contractor that will do some of the fine detail work. I'm done for now. I'll let you get back to- whatever."

Jesse nodded and he left. They just couldn't seem to manage a long conversation. Everything was down to business, and she couldn't quite seem to wedge in personal questions like "how do you stay so clean?" or "exactly how many navy blue sweaters do you own?" They never seemed to get anywhere close to that point.

Jesse just chalked it up to old man and continued working on her project. It took a few more hours but she was quite happy with the results. Although she'd never held the original amulet in her hands, she was fairly certain it was a reasonable facsimile. She couldn't judge the weight, but the characters and the color had been painstakingly matched. She had set the gem in the middle and the whole thing seemed to be as perfect as could be.

She wasn't in a hurry to talk to Pablo again, but it would definitely give her piece of mind to be able to hand over the whole check and have her rent taken care of, both the back rent and the next few months. That would give her time to finish her painting and possibly a few more on the same theme. She was sure that this painting would be picked up in the gallery. It was right up their alley and was the kind of thing that millennials loved to gobble up.

Jesse snapped a picture with her phone and then sent it off to the number on the front of Pablo's card. She had no idea how soon he would call, but just thinking about him sitting on her couch sipping that ridiculous cup of coffee suddenly gave her the urge to drink some coffee of her own. She put the amulet creation in the box with all the pictures except one. She planned to keep that for herself, just in case she ever got the urge to make a second one.

Coffee and a painting in the fall evening light, that's exactly what she was in the mood for. She grabbed an easel and a canvas and set them up outside. The air had a bit of a bite, but a sweat-shirt would take care of that. She'd paint another amulet-inspired painting. This one was beginning to take shape in her head already. Jesse went inside and grabbed the paints that she would need.

She had just finished putting a background base on the canvas when she heard a noise behind her. Pablo was standing at the garden door, holding up the crystal amulet to examine it in the fading light.

Jesse definitely knew that her door had been locked this time. Her throat tightened. Just who did this guy think he was? Never-mind. As soon as he handed over the money, she'd shoo him away and be done with him.

"There were some that doubted you could do the work. This is remarkable."

"Check, or are you going to put it on a card?" Jesse was even more anxious to get rid of him. His lemon suit had been discarded for a violet number. He was purple from head to toe, and Jesse really wanted to tell him that it wasn't his color.

"I'm sure that you could see it in your heart to do us one more favor, for another small fee, of course."

Jesse sighed. The only thing she wanted to do was get him out of there and call a locksmith to come change her locks.

"I'm a little too busy for any more commission pieces right now."

"This isn't a commission job. You see, the original of this piece was on loan to us, but has since been taken back by its owner. Your aunt was quite a friend of the steward of that particular collection."

"I don't see how any of this is relevant."

"But it is. Because we need you to do a subtle exchange."

Jesse's jaw dropped. "You mean you want me to steal it."

"Swap it, creative redistributing." He shrugged as if this was some minor detail to be overlooked. "Call it what you will. You did such an excellent job on this piece that I doubt anyone would ever notice."

"I'd notice. And there's a huge difference between making a copy with the intent of displaying it or studying it and making a forgery to swindle someone out of the real thing." Jesse had been worried about this, in the back of her head, that Pablo would use it as a forgery, passing it off as the real thing to some buyer down the road. With the debt hanging over her head, she'd pushed her fear aside, caveat emptor, let the buyer beware. Jesse had never imagined she'd be the one expected to complete the swindle.

"I think you've got the wrong person here," Jesse stammered.

"You are the only person. My organization has a policy of not involving outsiders in our business unless absolutely necessary. You have the required credentials and connections to complete the task."

"I'm not a thief."

"There you go with those dirty words again." Pablo shook his head. He wiggled his fingers and then made a fist. He was trying not to get agitated.

The promise of money was beginning to outweigh the danger of dealing with this off kilter asshole. He was a bully used to getting his way, and there was only one way to get rid of a bully.

"Look. I'm going to make this perfectly clear. Under no circumstances am I going to help you. Our business arrangement is over and I will not ever take another commision from you again. Please leave."

"Over?" Pablo stated. "You say it is over?" The look in his eye told Jesse that he wasn't used to being told no, and he definitely was the one that did all the breaking off of his relationships.

"Well then," Pablo said, loosening his violet tie. He pulled back his collar to reveal a nasty looking scar on his neck.

"You see this scar? You know where I got this scar? My wife. Are you surprised that I have a wife?" He didn't wait for an answer. He just ran his gloved fingers over the line on his throat. Even his gloves were violet. "She shot me, right in the throat. I thought I was dead. Thought I was gonna meet my maker, but then I woke up in the hospital. And I was alive, imagine that! My wife? They took her to jail. Then she begged and pleaded, 'oh sweetie, it was an accident. Big big accident. So sorry.'"

Pablo was slowly approaching, getting closer and closer to her, and Jesse found herself backing up to the edge of the garden, near to the gargoyle.

"She begged for me to take her back, drop charges, and I did. And nobody ever found her body."

There was no way of telling if he was just spinning a story or if he had just confessed to murder, and he probably knew that too. She didn't care. She just wanted this chubby short thug in violet to get out of her life forever.

"I can't. It's dishonest, and I don't care how much money-"

And that was it. Three steps forward and he shoved her toward the edge and she found herself toppling over the edge of the roof. For a split second, she thought he was trying to do one of those shake downs where the guy is hung over the side of the building and ends up caving or confessing after a few comedic moments. But Pablo had no intention of holding her there. One solid push and she was over, falling to her death.

There wasn't much of a life to flash before her eyes. She

closed them tight as the world rushed toward her. Then she didn't hit the ground. Someone grabbed her. Someone strong and hard, and they were flying.

Jesus Christ, she'd been rescued by Superman. Her eyes flew open. It was dark, but she was pretty damn sure she was in the arms of her very own gargoyle. He blinked at her and they rose, higher, back up to the rooftops.

"I told you. That guy is bad news, dammit."

It was Ray's voice that echoed back at her and for a moment, in his gravelly voice and steel gray eyes, she saw his face flicker, from fedora to fang face and back again. He set her down on a rooftop that overlooked their little garden. Pablo was already gone, but that didn't make Jesse feel any better. In fact, she was having a bit of a crisis trying to put everything together.

"Are you okay?" Raygoyle asked.

"Yes. No. What the hell?"

"Stay here."

"Wait!" But it was too late. Her gargoyle had already spread his wings and was gliding down to the garden below. Somewhere along the way he'd picked up a large iron bar and was wielding it as he headed into her apartment.

She closed her eyes, blinking hard to clear her vision. It hadn't been a trick of her mind. His whole form was flashing between Ray and the gargoyle. Then she got mad. That bastard Pablo had just tried to kill her. She needed her own iron bar to take out his knees and maybe that smug grin on his face. Rat bastard. She turned and saw there was a strangely familiar garden behind her. It was similar to the layout of the one below, though this one had only one door leading off of it. She tried the door. It was locked. Great, she was stuck on top of the building until he came and got her.

Her gargoyle. Her flying gargoyle. Who was also Ray.

What. The. Fuck.

She heard the flap of wings and turned around to see Ray

standing behind her. He was back in fedora form, but he was flickering.

"Your funky old man is on the fritz." It was a lame thing to say, but what else could she add.

"Not really. It's just a perception filter. The more you know what I look like, the less it actually works on you. I- Olivia was supposed to tell you everything."

"Well, she didn't."

"I know."

They stood there for a moment in an awkward silence.

"He's gone, by the way. You want to go back to your apartment?" Ray asked.

"He tried to kill me," Jesse answered, incredulously.

"I saw that."

"Why?"

"I told you he was bad news. Are you ready to go back now?" he asked again.

"I need a gun."

"No, you don't."

"I'm going to shoot that bastard in the neck. Not like his wife. He's going to die. With prejudice. And…"

Ray was grinning at her.

"And why do you think this is amusing? He just tried to kill me and you're sitting there smiling."

"I don't know. I'm kinda used to people screaming and trying to run away. You know, like, 'Ahh. Ahh, he's a monster. He's gonna eat me!'"

"I'm pretty sure if you were going to eat me, you would have done it by now. I mean you just saved my life."

"Are you ready to go back?"

"He has keys to my apartment. He just let himself in."

"I threw the deadbolts. I'm not stupid. And I'll rekey the elevator. No one will be able to get up without a retina scan and a fingerprint."

Jesse glanced at his hands.

"That would work for you?"

"I have retinas and fingerprints." He held up his chunky hands. "They may look clumsy, but I'm quite good with my hands."

Jesse blinked. Was her gargoyle flirting with her?

"Okay."

"Okay, you want it done or okay you want to go back to the other roof?"

"Yes."

Without any other warning, Ray scooped her up in his arms, spread his wings and strode off the edge of the building. They didn't so much as fly down as float, or perhaps glide. She wrapped her hands tightly around his neck and once down, he folded his wings about them.

"Are you going to put me down now?" she asked.

He didn't say anything. He just sort of looked at her funny. She touched his skin. It was cool to the touch but soft under the rippled stony gray skin.

"How do you work, anyway?" she inquired.

He set her down, but he didn't let her go. She tilted her head up to look at him. He was taller than she had realized, probably because he'd been sitting down for most of her life. It also made sense that Ray always wore a fedora. It was tall and wide enough to give him the illusion of being shorter.

Her fingers stroked his neck, almost absently, getting the feel of him as a man, not as a stone statue.

"It makes more sense now," she said. "How you could demolish a bathroom in a day, and be completely spotless and sweat-free minutes later."

Still he said nothing. He just stared at her mouth. She'd begun to stare at his. It was wide and he clearly had fangs, but what kind of kisser would he be? What would it feel like to press into his cool skin? Did he have a tongue? Of course he had a tongue. How could he talk without a tongue?

He lowered his head and she tilted her chin up to meet his kiss. It was hot and demanding and sent sparks down to her toes. His tongue swept into her mouth and her knees threatened to buckle.

There was a pounding. Was it in her head? No, it was at her door. She broke off the kiss.

"Oh God. That's the door. I should get it. Do you have a bat?"

That statement didn't seem to amuse him. He headed toward the door.

"Ray. Is that really your name? Ray? Wait up! Aren't you afraid of someone seeing you like that?" She trailed after him.

"No, that's not how it works."

"How what works?"

Ray peered through the peephole on the door. "Who the hell is that?"

"Well, move over and let me look." She squeezed passed him

Behind the door, she could see a rather nervous looking Luis. He wasn't making any qualms about hiding the baseball bat in his hands.

She threw back the dead bolts and opened the door.

"Who's that?" both Ray and Luis asked at nearly the same time. From his reaction, Jesse could tell that Luis was indeed seeing Ray the old man, not the gray monster.

"Ray, Luis. Luis, Ray." she introduced.

"What are you planning on doing with the bat, Luis?" Ray said.

Luis tried to tuck the bat behind his back.

"My boys told me that the blue boy was back."

Jesse smiled. "You didn't actually have to keep an eye on me."

"We ain't keeping an eye on you. We're keeping an eye on

our street. You know, head off problems before they get into the family bodega and practice their little five finger discounts."

Except Luis and a bat was probably no match for Pablo. She'd have no problem believing that Pablo carried several guns beneath that smooth exterior of a suit.

"I appreciate the effort, but I swear, I'm okay. And I don't plan on him ever returning again either." As far as Pablo knew, she was a flat pancake, though he'd probably wondered why there wasn't a huge scene around her corpse as he left the building.

"How do you know where she lives?" Ray said pointedly.

"He's got a side hustle," said Jesse. "He does deliveries at the bodega sometimes."

"And who's he?" Luis squinted at Ray.

"He's my grandpa."

Ray let out a huff, but said nothing more. He squinted back at Luis. "That fool in the suit tried to kill her today, so I appreciate the extra eyes."

Luis glanced back at Jesse to confirm.

"Tried to throw me off the roof, but Ray--er, Grandpa heard and stopped him."

"Are you shittin' me? And you just let him walk? I would have broken this bat over his fuckin' head."

"I know you would have, Luis, but what else could an old man have done?"

"Neither one of you called the po-po?"

He looked at Ray, eyeballing the old man from head to toe, expecting him to be the type with the police on speed dial.

"I prefer to deal with my issues in-house," Ray said.

Was that a little light of appreciation glimmering in Luis's eyes?

"I got you. I got you. Jesse, you need anything, you just call for delivery. We'll come real fast."

"Thank you, Luis."

"Yes. Thank you," Ray said. He backed up and grabbed a sticky note off the counter. "But if you see them again, call this number first. These are some scary, scary guys, and I don't think a baseball bat will do much if you don't catch them by surprise, put them down on the ground first. If they see you coming, they'll shoot first."

"Got it. Be sneaky or pack my own heat," Luis said with a nod.

"Don't you dare get shot, Luis," Jesse warned.

"Aww, you care that much? Eh?"

Luis's phone rang and he answered. Jesse could hear rapid-fire Spanish out the other end. He rolled his eyes and saluted with the bat, giving her one last wink before heading down the elevator.

Jesse closed the door and relocked the two deadbolts. She went to sit down on the couch. With his wings folded away, tucked tight against his body, Ray sat on the other end of the couch, as if he did so every day.

There was another awkward silence.

Good God, were they back to that?

"I'm going back to my place to get a start on the elevator," he said as he stood up.

"I- okay," was Jesse's only response.

He left the door to the garden open on his way out. She figured he wanted to be able to hear if she had any more unexpected visitors.

Jesse had so many questions floating around in her head. She felt like the whole world was spinning. Maybe she should write them down. No, they weren't ordered enough yet. She needed to paint. Jesse stepped out onto the garden patio and waited for the panic of nearly falling to overwhelm her. Nothing. She felt safe, ready even to work on her painting.

The gargoyle statue was back. Had he already gone back into being a statue? Was it a night time sun thing? She shook her head. She'd definitely seen Ray in the day and the night, so it was something he could control.

Jesse walked over and poked the statue. It fizzled and wiggled, like she was touching reflection, but she met with nothing solid.

He had a hologram… of himself, to cover when he was covered with a hologram of Ray. Her gargoyle was becoming more mysterious the more she learned.

❧ 8 ❧

FRELINRAY

Jesse was cool, calm and collected. Ray was ready to tear chunks out of the wall and hurl them down on the unsuspecting asshole that had decided to mess with Jesse. No, that was too distant, too cold. He wanted to grab a hold on that chunky pastel asshole and fly him up to the top of his limit and drop him, watching his pretty corpse make a big red splotch on the pavement. They'd pick him up with a mop. No, there'd be too many questions. He'd have to drop him in the river. He'd be one more suicide in a long line of floating corpses.

How was she so calm? She was already out there painting. The moment he realized she'd gone over the edge, he'd sprung into action out of shear fear. He hadn't cared who saw or what cameras might have picked him up as he swooped down, caught her and flown to his safety spot.

When he'd bought the buildings in the 1940's, he'd walled off the top floor of the tallest one. There was literally no way to get to it unless one had wings. Of course now, someone could probably land a small helicopter anywhere they pleased, but back then, he'd been sure that if Rose ever came looking for him again, he'd have a safe place at least to gather his thoughts and mount a defense from.

He'd grown too complacent, set down too many roots. Olivia had not been one that wanted to move. He'd fought her over it more than once but always been on the losing side. Go, she had said, but she was staying.

He had no intention of ever leaving her side again. Now, he had Jesse to think of. And he couldn't stop thinking of her. He hadn't meant to claim a kiss, but he did not regret it, couldn't regret what still burned on his lips and drove him crazy even now. And yet she'd just gone to answer the door as if she kissed him every day.

Part of him was rejoicing though. She didn't think he was a monster. In fact, she'd pretty easily accepted his form as fact. He knew she had questions, but sitting still was not much of an option for him. He had to keep busy to keep from wrapping his wings around her and spreading her legs with his tail so that he could plunge hilt deep into her with his hard cock.

When she came in from painting, she brewed them a pot of tea and asked him to sit down on the couch like a civilized couple carrying on a perfectly normal conversation. It was Olivia's couch, so it was hardy enough for him to sit comfortably and not worry about snapping the legs if he gave it his full weight.

"I have a list," Jessie said.

He smiled. There was something cute about her making a list.

She held up a hand and ticked off fingers. "First of all, how old are you? And are you an alien or a mutant? And do you actually turn to stone? Why? How? And is Ray your real name? I mean, you don't exactly look like a Ray."

Ray held a finger and she stopped talking.

"A long time ago, in a galaxy far, far away," he started.

"Yeah, I've heard that one before. Try again," she chuckled.

"It's true though. A very long - centuries long - time ago, my planet was at war with another, and many ships were sent out to look for supplies or alternative options for settlements."

"And you landed here."

"We crashed here. Most of us didn't survive. Those that did tried to make peace with the humans, but our leader and his negotiation party were slaughtered. That's when we decided that 'hide and wait' would be our best option of survival."

"Hide in plain sight. As statues," Jesse said, nodding.

"We have the ability to stone sleep. Durammna, we call it. To rest and turn ourselves to living stone. Some can turn only parts of themselves to stone at will. I can't really."

"All or nothing, eh?"

It felt good to get everything out in the open, to explain and stop hiding himself from Jesse.

"How many of you are there?" she asked.

"I don't know how many are left. At least a dozen, I think. We scattered. And some decided not to wait. They claimed a mate, started a family and lived their life without stone sleep."

"They mated? They, you can do that?"

She still had no clue just how much he burned to do that.

"I almost did. I would have. Jessenia. But she died. I haven't felt the urge since-"

"My aunt. Great aunt. You were going to mate with her?"

"The Rose Syndicate, they captured me and by the time I escaped, she was gone, and Olivia and Margaret were all alone. I took them in, and we came here. Been here ever since. Olivia didn't want to leave."

"Olivia loved this place. I do too," Jesse said.

"The Rose knows I'm here. It won't be safe for either of us if they are determined. They obviously weren't after me. Otherwise, they would have sent in a strike team to grab me off the roof."

"They wanted me to make that amulet thing. And trade it,

steal it." Jesse stood up and fetched a picture. Ray recognized it immediately.

"It's a sigil."

"A what?"

"Sigil. It's sort of a com link and transporter built into one."

"Transporter. Like Beam me Up Scottie?"

"Similar, but it doesn't work unless there's a master beacon in orbit around the planet and as far as I know that's at the bottom of the Atlantic. Besides, there's no one out there to do the transporting. Our ship was destroyed, and there's no way to build another one that's capable of opening a wormhole back home."

Jesse was getting a rather glazed look in her eyes, as if she was having trouble processing all the information he'd just given to her.

"So why did they want me to swap a fake for a real one? Pablo said it was because they'd recently lost access to a real one, but couldn't he have just had one stolen?"

"I don't know. I'll have to ask my source," he said.

"You have a source?"

"I have a source."

"Is he an alien too?"

"Not that I know of."

"Then I'm coming with you."

⚜ *9* ⚜

JESSE

This place was weird. Not only was it weird, but her entire life had suddenly turned weird. One minute she'd been an artist living in New York City and the next she was on the hunt for information at an alternative night club about an alien artifact and lusting over the alien it had once belonged to. Not to mention that he'd flown her down the side of the building, after being shoved off by a Rose Syndicate hitman, into the alley in order to keep her apartment locked and bolted from the inside in case they decided to go poking around again. They must be suspicious by now as to why she hadn't either been reported dead or called the police to report Pablo.

There were people of all types here, and everyone was letting their freak flag fly. She'd seen more than one person with horns and one guy had piercings in places Jesse didn't realize were possible. Others were tattooed or made up nearly beyond recognition as human beings. It was the perfect place for an alien to hide or at least get a drink without anyone paying the slightest attention.

Ray had turned off his device thingy so apparently everyone

59

else could see his true form. One woman paused to stroke his wings and Jesse was surprised at her own desire to punch that woman in the face. She must have noticed because she backed off, hands up in apology.

Ray motioned for her to sit at the bar. The bartender paused and gave her the once over. Was she too normal looking? Should she have put some color in her hair? Not that she could match the blue spikes of his mohawk or the perfectly drawn cat eyes under his red rimmed glasses.

"What can I get for you?"

"Something sweet, but funky," Jesse stated.

"I got you. I got you." He didn't ask Ray what he wanted. The bartender turned and mixed and returned with a neon purple concoction for her and a whiskey, neat for Ray.

"Twice in a week. I'm glad you've been taking my advice," the bartender said.

Jesse took a sip from her drink. The thing was a perfect concoction of sweet and sour, cold and salty. She nodded, smiling, as the alcohol kicked in.

"Good, eh? What's your name, sweetie?" he said, flashing a smile himself. Ray didn't seem as friendly.

"Pablo tried to dump her off a roof," Ray told him, getting right to the point.

"I see. I think I might have discovered why Rose is all hot to trot about your little thing."

Wait, was Jesse the little thing in this set?!

"They started blinking," the bartender said, leaning over the bar as if were telling a great secret.

"Blinking," Ray said. He didn't sound very credulous.

"Blinking?" Jesse repeated.

"Blinking." The bartender leaned back to gauge Ray's reaction. Ray's hand tightened so hard onto the edge of the bar that his claws dug into the wood.

"Hey, easy on the furniture."

"Sorry. Are you sure? I've been waiting for that blasted thing to blink for over a thousand years."

"What can I tell you? That's the rumor on the street."

"Clue me in, please," Jesse said. The punch was beginning to hit her, but she didn't think that she'd drunk enough to be this confused.

"The sigil," Ray began. "If it blinks, it means it's activated. If it's activated it means two things. First of all, someone has either fished the beacon out of the Atlantic or constructed a new one. Secondly, it means that someone out there has come to retrieve us."

"You mean there's an alien ship out there?" Giles asked, eyes growing wide as they glanced upward.

"Giles, they'll be camouflaged and shielded against detection. And they won't come down. It's against the code. They'll bring us up."

Jesse sat silent for a moment. Ray was leaving. Leaving Earth. He was going home and leaving her to herself. If he left, was there any guarantee that the Rose Syndicate would leave her alone? Would she be safe once he went back to his space ship in the sky?

"How long do you have?" she asked him suddenly.

She meant, how long do we have? How much time did she have before she was completely alone in the world?

"I don't know. I'd have to gain access to a sigil."

"Don't you have one?" the bartender asked.

"I did. But the Rose Syndicate stole it when they captured me. It must have been destroyed when-" Ray broke off and looked down, shaking his head. "Otherwise I would have known that it had gone active. We're attuned to only one, but we can activate any that we find."

"So you have to locate one and then check it to see," Giles said.

"Yes."

Giles produced a piece of paper from under the bar. He wrote down an address.

"Then I suppose it's quite lucky that there's been a rumor of a man coming and going from this office. He's overly fond of pastel suits," he said, handing the paper to Ray.

Jesse took the paper before Ray could grab it. "Thanks," she said.

"You're welcome. And you, pretty lady, are welcome in here anytime."

"Jesse. Give it to me," Ray said quietly.

"Don't be rude. Drink your whiskey," she replied. She finished off her concoction and to his credit, Ray reached for the glass and drank his own. She put the sticky note in her bra.

"You owe me a dance," Jesse said. Ray looked at her like she had three heads.

"I don't-"

"Oh, come on. It's easy. Just grab ahold of my hips and sway."

"But-"

"No buts."

She wasn't sure where this compulsion was coming from, but she wanted, needed to be close to him. She placed his hands on her hips and looped her arms around his neck. There was a slower song playing. She didn't recognize it, but it was easy enough to dance to.

"See? This is nice, isn't it?" Jesse leaned up against him. It hadn't occurred to her that in his true form he was wearing little else than an old looking pair of ragged biker shorts. There was definitely something bulging from them.

"Ray?" She pressed up tighter against him. Yes, that was a definite hard on. Her gargoyle had the hots for her. He had the hots for her and he was leaving. Nothing in this life was fair.

But that didn't have to stop her from living out one fantasy in particular.

"You know, I think it's time we went somewhere a little more secluded."

That was all the suggestion needed before they were out the door. Ray turned his camo back on and in no time flat, they were in the back alley behind the apartment building. He pulled her up into his arms and the two of them flew back up to the rooftop garden.

"I don't think I'll ever get used to flying," Jesse said when her feet were back on the ground.

"I miss it. It's too dangerous to do it very often in the city. Someone might see. Plus, your technology has had a serious boost in the past ten years. I'm never sure if I'm on the edge or not. Government services like to keep tech back from the public sector."

Jesse imagined Ray soaring in a field, doing loop de loops like a boss. She still hadn't uncoupled her arms from around his neck, and he didn't seem to be in a hurry to do anything else. Ray put his hands back on her hips and the two of them swayed back and forth to some unheard song.

"I want you," Ray said.

A spark of anticipation flew across her skin. Somehow she'd always known, despite the grumpy old man camouflage, that this gargoyle was destined to be hers. Through those summer nights when she slept out on the roof as a child to the moment he rescued her to certain death, all the moments were leading to the simple fact that she wanted him just as badly as he wanted her. Whether for a few weeks or a few hours, she wasn't going to let anything stand in the way of that basic need.

She tilted her head up and offered her mouth. He claimed it in a searing kiss. He pulled her in closer, wrapping his wings around the two of them. She had thought the bulge in his pants was large at the club. It was huge now. She lowered her hand to stroke him through the material. Jesse wanted to take out that cock and thoroughly examine it. To see what a stone alien member might look like, what it would feel like on her tongue and inside her.

Ray broke off the kiss and started to stammer. "I just want to warn you. I've not… it's been. I haven't-"

Jesse finally interpreted what he was trying to say.

"So you haven't had sex since 1940?" Jesse tried to do the math in her head. Eighty or so years was a long time for a dry spell.

"Times were different back then. Jessenia and I, we never… There was very little sex before marriage for a proper girl. We were going to get married when her father returned, but he didn't make it through Dunkirk, and I was captured."

"So you and Aunt Olivia never-"

"No. Olivia was more like a daughter, or a sister. I never felt an attraction other than affection for her. And Midge was a rebellious little brat." It was always nice to know that the alien you were about to fuck didn't have the hots for your grandmother.

"So before Jessenia?" she asked.

"My species do not feel compelled to mate with every female with an attractive rack that walks by. We are more selective. It is not just in our society, it's in our nature. When we meet a compatible female, a gland in our mouth prepares. We can feel it swell and-"

"Is that the only thing that swells?" Her hand returned to his bulge, as if she hadn't inspected it before.

"No. I believe that our species are similar in that matter."

"Well, I will say that it's been a long time for me too. Just not a thousand years long."

Since college when everything was one big experiment. She'd hooked up with several guys, but finding one amongst the art crowd just hadn't worked out. And moving to New York hadn't lent itself to the dating scene either. Online computers were cold and calculating, but this was something different. He was right in front of her, hard in her hand, and she was not going to pass it up, even if he was leaving the planet soon.

Jesse was glad that she had put on something more formal than a pair of paint splattered jeans and an old t-shirt for their trip to Evensong.

She unbuttoned a few buttons and then pulled the rest of the top off over her head. She could swear that Ray had stopped breathing.

"Do you want to touch me?" she asked.

"More than anything."

She reached back and unfastened her bra. "Then touch me." That was the last bit of encouragement Ray needed to step forward and cup her breasts. He dipped his head to put her nipple in his mouth, playing over the tip of it with his tongue.

Jesse unbuttoned her skirt and slid it down with her panties. Ray's hands and mouth were all over her body, exploring, tasting and pleasuring until she nearly fell over.

"My turn."

Ray stopped and stood up straight, giving her permission to touch and stroke his fine muscled abs, feel the leathery skin of his wings, and finally back to his cock. With a tug at the strange material he wore, she set it free to marvel at it. She knelt in front of him.

In general shape and size, it was close to a human cock, except the largest she had ever seen. It had a pronounced head with three ridges on the staff just below. Further down, there were little raised bumps, like those built into fancy dildos.

"Your cock looks made to please a girl."

"Is that not the objective?" Ray smiled down at her as she ran a finger along the bumps and ridges. He stopped smiling when she reached out with her tongue to give his head a little taste. That was all the encouragement she needed to take his entire head into her mouth.

Ray groaned and his hand tangled in her hair. Part of her wanted him to take control, to fuck her mouth and fill it with alien spunk. The other half knew that if he did that, she'd probably have to wait to get fucked, and she was not in a waiting mood. She was already hot and wet and waiting.

She let go of his cock and stood up. She grabbed his hand and guided it to her pussy. His fingers wasted no time exploring her wet folds and finding that pleasure center that buckled her knees.

"Yes, that's it, take your pleasure. I want to feel it." Ray whispered and he pushed a finger up inside her. His other hand pulled her to him, supported her as she crested the wave of orgasm. He waited for a moment, but both of them knew that one was not going to be enough for her. She would not be truly satisfied until he was inside her.

He guided her over to the stone bench on one edge of the garden. He sat down, straddling the bench and guided her onto his lap, straddling him. His cock stood tall and proud between her legs, so close to its goal.

She nodded and Ray lifted her, pausing a moment at her entrance, before slowly lowering her onto his towering member.

"Yes." It was complete heaven. She'd never dreamed of being this full of someone, alien or not. He was fully inside her, waiting, so patiently for her to adjust. It didn't take long.

"Fuck me now." It was a moot point of who was fucking whom, since she was on top, but his hands were essential in giving her enough lift to come nearly off of him and then down again, deliciously full and slick, even against the friction of his perfectly sculpted ridges.

She rode him, and when she couldn't continue the thrusts because of the pleasure, he assisted and pushed her even further.

"I'm going to-" he finally spat out.

"Yes. Fuck yes," It wasn't the most intelligible answer, but she gave him the permission he needed to bury his cock inside her one last time and with a guttural moan, take his own pleasure.

10

FRELINRAY

The address that Giles had given him was on the twenty-seventh floor of an office building. It was loaded with cameras and Ray could see no way to case the place without being spotted. Sure, he could fly up and smash a window, but that would draw too much attention and it didn't guarantee that Rose would close up shop and disappear into the ether the next day.

"We could get Luis to do it," Ray suggested.

"Luis is already close enough to trouble because of me. This is my turn. It'll be fine," Jesse told him.

"I never realized how much Olivia's studio was like a one woman counterfeit shop," Jesse said as she printed out a laminated badge. She'd already put the finishing touches on her outfit and soon stood there like an overworked, underpaid cleaning lady.

"One doesn't stay under the radar without learning a few tricks of the trade," Ray said. It was useful to have someone who could keep up with documentation that proved he wasn't a thousand years old, and Olivia had been good with the artistic eye for just the right amount of truth mixed with the lies. Ray still didn't like this plan. It was dangerous and he'd told her so, but she was intent on seeing it through.

"I'll be in and out in a few minutes. Just enough to take a look around and then, poof, I'll be back downstairs. You obviously can't go. They'd catch you in an instant."

Jesse could do it. No one looked twice at a maid. She could grab the trash and in a few minutes of looking around, get a very good idea of what they were dealing with.

But if Pablo was there, he may very well want to try and finish the job he failed to complete the other day, and Ray would not be there to stop them. Chances were that at 8:00 PM, the place would be deserted and everyone would be just fine.

That didn't stop the tingling sense of doubt.

Jesse approached him. He loved the way that she rubbed her hands along his chest and followed the line of his muscles around his hips. She tested the firmness of his ass with her hands.

"So tell me... Why do you only wear this little shorts number? I mean it's hot and all, but isn't it a little impractical?"

"What's impractical is going into stone sleep with any clothes on. They don't change with me. This fabric does. It's the last bit that I have. Besides, have you ever tried to put on a sweater with wings? That is impractical."

"So the people on your planet don't actually wander around with such little clothing?"

"I'm sorry to disappoint you." He said with a laugh. She did look disappointed, but only for a moment. Then she went back to fondling his cock again.

"So we have an hour or two," she hinted. Yes, they'd both agreed it was better to wait until after sundown. Then he would have the cover of darkness just in case the shit hit the fan. But that was not what he wanted to think about while her hand stroked his cock.

He popped the buttons on her shirt one by one, taking care

not to rip them off. It wouldn't do to waste her time sewing them back on. Her sports bra flummoxed him. It flattened her luscious curves and he had no idea how to get that thing off. He went for the zipper on her trousers instead. She giggled, but let him proceed. Jesse's hand was not still. She was busy outlining his cock, tracing her way down the length of one side and back up the other.

Ray slid her trousers down and cupped her ass with his hands. He tested the weight and then pulled her closer to him.

"Why don't you take off your short shorts?" Jesse hinted.

"I will if you take off that contraption hiding your breasts."

She laughed and pushed back from him. With a few miraculous twists of her arms, she was free of it. She turned around and put his hands on her breasts. His fingers found her nipples. They were hard but got even more pointed as he played with them.

"Is that better?" she asked.

"Mmm, yes." His cock pressed forward, finding the fold between her ass cheeks.

"But you haven't held up your end of the bargain," she teased.

"You grabbed my hands. How am I supposed to take off any more when my hands are busy?"

"Okay, you can remove your hands for a moment."

He never knew he needed permission, but he quickly shucked down his pants and then on his way back to her breasts, pulled her panties down to mid thigh.

It was plenty enough for his cock to find friction and come to full attention. He stood there, for a long minute, plucking at her nipples, stretching his wings and rubbing against her delicious backside. Then suddenly, it wasn't enough.

His hand wandered lower and slid between her lips to find her clit.

"You are so wet for me," he noted.

"Self defense. That cock of yours is so big, my body has to

prepare itself. And-" she was going to say more, but her voice broke off in a moan and he increased the stroke. Oh, hells he wanted to possess her completely. It would be so easy, to bite her now, to claim her, but instinctively, he knew she wasn't ready for that. There was too much unknown in the equation. He'd have to be content with just the simple pleasures of making her orgasm and feeling her body ripple over his.

He held her close, for she was already almost to that point, ready to cum. He pressed into her.

"What is that?" she asked, surprised.

He froze. "What?"

"It's not your cock and it's not your finger."

"My tail."

He gave it a thrust to exemplify. She seemed to like it.

"Oh! You have a tail? Oh God, that's quite a tail. Oh fuck."

She bent over but his hands held her steady as she rode her first orgasm. He waited, until she was just on the end of wave before withdrawing his tail and swiveling her around. With a steady movement, he picked her up and placed her down onto his cock. She let out a moan of approval and he settled her there, letting her adjust to the new fullness. His tail, now no longer occupied, slid along her back to her inviting ass.

"You are going to?"

"If you want."

"Do it."

He pressed his tail into her, filling both of her holes. He began thrusting, lifting her off his cock while he filled her ass with his tail, then dropping her back down on his cock. He breathed deeply to avoid spilling himself immediately as her body clenched him and she moaned from deep in her chest. His movements became more frantic, more determined as she screamed out her pleasure and he finally pulled her to him and let out a moan of his own while his cock emptied itself inside her.

He held her, still fully impaled, until their hearts slowed and their breathing returned to normal.

"How come you hid this tail from me before?"

"I normally keep it curled up. The perception filter doesn't really work with it. And I think it would be silly to see Ray, the grumpy old man, with a tail flashing behind him."

"It's pretty adept."

Ray smiled. "That it is. And you know what? It doesn't you know, need to cum. Sometime, I'll have to show you how I can fuck you for hours with it."

"Hours, eh? I'm lucky to be able to walk after one."

Ray smiled and lifted her down onto the ground. To emphasize her point, Jesse walked off to the bathroom, bowlegged.

11

JESSE

J esse couldn't stop the theme music from *Mission Impossible* from playing in her head as she put on her headphones and headed in the service entrance of the building with her bag of cleaning supplies. She had a curly mop of a wig on her head that hopefully gave her a more ethnic look, and she'd done everything to de-emphasize her curves. She was just another boring woman getting about her day and cleaning up the mess of her betters.

The whole stereotype irked Jesse, but this was not the time for a social crusade. This was Operation Figure Out What the Assholes Were Up To.

Getting into the building was easy enough. No one looked twice as she headed in right behind a group of three other cleaning people, and no one questioned her as she got in the elevator and hit the button for the twenty-sixth floor.

They'd agreed it was safer to take the stairs up to the last floor. The elevator might alert someone getting out on the floor, but it was less likely they had also rigged the stairs.

Up the stairs, she listened at the fire door for any sounds. Everything seemed quiet.

"How is it going?" Ray whispered in her ears.

"I'm not there yet, hold your horses." Jesse opened the door and peeked out. No one in sight. So far so good. She was in a hallway with four doors, each one labeled with a neat little plaque.

"Shit. There are four of them. How am I supposed to know which one is the right one?" There was silence over the headphones. Great. She looked at the four plaques. The first one sounded like a law firm. It was almost too boring. But maybe that's what they were supposed to sound like.

The second was Bright Inc., the third Compass Unlimited, and the finally one was Smith Industries. She read the titles out loud to Ray.

"Compass. Compass Rose," he repeated. "If it's a travel agency, it's the perfect cover. Go with that one."

Jesse nodded out of habit, even though she realized that he couldn't see her. It sounded logical enough. She ran the card through the lock and like magic, it opened. Ray had given her the card and told her it would open nearly any card lock on the planet. She'd taken it with a grain of salt since he'd been so proud of inventing it, but sure enough it clicked open.

Jesse pushed the door open and entered a rather nondescript office. There was a receptionist's desk and a few impersonal cubicles, but none of them sported any personal pictures or calendars with dates. It was as if a bunch of robots filled those seats and worked in the boxes. Of course, the company could have a no personal stuff policy, but there wasn't so much as a potted plant to spice up the place.

"This is the place," Jesse said after studying the office for another minute.

"You are sure?"

"Really. I'm staring at a roll of red ribbon. You know. Like the one used to wrap the box that I was given."

She pulled out her phone and started taking snapshots.

Perhaps there was something in office that she could use. She circled around to the other side of the desk. In the chair, there was a large package envelope wrapped with red ribbon. But that's not what caught her attention.

"Oh. Shit." She grabbed the envelop just to make sure. It was definitely addressed to her. It even had a little neon green sticky note on it.

"What?" Ray asked.

"He knows."

"Who knows what."

"Pablo knows I'm here. He left a package here for me. There's a note on it. It says, 'Jesse, I hope you reconsider my offer.'"

"Time to go."

Jesse's mind was whirling, but she definitely agreed. It was time to get the heck out of dodge. Screw the stairs, she was grabbing the elevator.

It seemed like a lifetime as she waited for it to ding and open. She headed straight down to the lobby. From there, she'd only be a few steps away from Ray and a quick getaway.

The elevator dinged and stopped on the seventeenth floor. She looked down and pretended to fiddle with her cleaning supplies, hoping her curly mop of a wig would hide her from the man whose identity was clear. Mint green was today's theme, and the white slim tie made Jesse want to reach out and strangle him with it.

"So have you?" he said as soon as the doors closed. It was clear that he knew exactly who she was, who she'd been the whole time.

"Why should I when you tried to kill me?"

"You took the envelope. And it was pretty clear you weren't actually going to die, wasn't it? If I wanted you to die I would have slit your throat."

"All the details are in the envelope?" she asked.

"Of course. I'm glad we could do business together in a more civilized manner."

The elevator hit the second floor, and Jesse walked straight up to the doors. Slick as you please, she pulled out her taser and put a few volts into the bastard. It was so satisfying to watch him jiggle, jump and slump, it was nearly as good as actually killing him.

"You. Do not throw me off a roof again. Ever. Are we clear?"

Pablo could only manage a moan. The door opened and Jesse pushed the button to the top floor. She stepped out, quickly and the doors closed. No one stopped her as she exited the building and swiftly walked around the corner where Ray joined her.

"He bugged my apartment. That's the only way he could know. He was ready for us. Knew everything."

"Did you tase him? Is that what I heard?"

"I was going to stab him, but I didn't have any scissors handy."

"Jesse. He's dangerous. And now you've wounded his pride."

Jesse stopped dead on the sidewalk and turned to glare at Ray.

"He tried to kill me then backtracked it. Seriously. He's lucky I didn't kick him in the balls while he was down." Jesse thought about that a second more and restarted her walk. "Why the hell didn't I kick him in the balls!"

Ray just sighed.

"You got some magic gizmo that can check for bugs, because I'm pretty sure my entire apartment is infested."

"I have something, yes. But it's not magic. It's technology."

"Magic, technology, I don't care as long as it works."

"It should. But until then, I'll take you up to the safe house. It should be more secure."

He gave her little warning before he scooped her up and with a flap and a flying leap, quickly took her high into the sky.

Jesse wasn't sure how Lois Lane did it, got used to having a boyfriend who could grab her off the street and take her high into the air.

He put her down on top of the building that he'd taken her to right after he'd rescued her that first time. The one with the locked door. Ray put her down and then placed his hand on the door. It clicked open and he waved for her to enter.

As they entered, it lit up. Lights were necessary because there were no windows, and as Jesse scouted the place, no doors either. Otherwise, the place was cleanly furnished in mostly the color scheme of black and white. There was a bedroom that harkened back to an earlier time with a cream bedspread and a slightly girly finish, but it was generic enough that it probably hadn't belonged to a girl for long. There was a second room, originally intended as a bedroom, but now was stocked to the gills with canned and dry goods, a veritable bunker of food stuffs for a siege.

"You've created your own secret annex. Does one of those bookcases hide a stairway down?"

"No. I walled it all off years ago. The stairs below too. Completely sealed off from both ends. The only way to get into this apartment is through that door, and the only way to get through that door is to fly. It was a lot more secure before they developed helicopters and drones, but it is better than nothing. That door is also biometrically sealed. I can add you to the configuration.

"You aren't going to leave me up here, are you?"

"Just until I can sweep your apartment."

"And if you die, I won't be able to escape. I'll be stuck up here like Rapunzel."

"If I die, you have a cell phone. Call the police or fire department. I'm sure they'll be able to locate the staircase and dig you out in a day or two. I'll bring your canvas up. You can paint while you wait. Does that sound nice?"

How could he sound so caring and condescending at the same time? "Ray."

"I'll be right back."

And with that, he had run up to the patio and jumped over the side of the building.

It was late, and she was getting grumpy. Ray by default had probably been nocturnal, but she needed her sleep. At least there was a bed here. She hadn't spotted one at his apartment, and her little twin bed wasn't going to fit the two of them. The double in the room was going to be a tight squeeze, but she was sure that they could manage.

It was funny, how she and Ray had yet to manage making love in a bed. She had nothing to complain about from the previous times, but it was just unusual how they had avoided the bed. Jesse rolled her eyes at herself. A minute ago, she'd been tired and ready to sleep. Now she could feel her body readying itself for some alien cock.

His tail was no joke either.

Jesse unbuttoned her shirt and her pants. Knowing her luck, she'd be stuck on top of this building in one of the ugliest outfits ever. No, she wouldn't let her thoughts go there. That would mean that Ray was not coming back to her. She pulled off her shirt and shucked down her pants, leaving everything in a rumpled pile at the end of the bed. With a smirk, she pulled off her sports bra, remembering how disconcerting Ray had found it earlier. Just in her panties, she sat on the bed. She waited. Jesse had not confirmed how long he was going to be gone.

The possibility of getting mounted had her squirming too much to sleep now.

What about the envelope? She'd left it with the cleaning supplies as she'd come through the door. She hopped up from the bed and went to grab it.

Ray must have already thought about it, because he'd taken it with him. Damn him. Not that she could do much about it now.

She rolled her eyes and grabbed her phone.

Ray picked it up almost immediately.

"Are you almost done?" she asked.

"Nearly."

"Have you found anything?"

"I'll discuss that with you later." Jesse interpreted that as he wasn't sure if he was still being overheard so he was being intentionally vague.

"Fine, but I'm getting impatient."

"Some things take time."

"I'm sitting up here, by myself and I'm only wearing a pair of panties. How ever am I supposed to amuse myself?"

She practically heard him harden on the phone. "I'll be there soon." He hung up the phone and Jesse sauntered back into the bedroom. She lay in the center of the bed and struck what she hoped was a sexy pose. Two minutes later, she heard the door open.

Ray stood in the bedroom doorway for a long minute.

"Are you waiting for an invitation?" She asked.

"Just taking in the view. That was not very nice, you know. It's possible they've bugged your phone as well."

"And whose goddamn business is it if I'm having wild sex with a consenting adult? Because you know they must have heard all that monkey sex earlier."

Ray approached the bed. "You mean when you screamed how much you loved getting fucked by my cock and my tail at the same time?"

"Exactly. I'm sure it's no secret how much I adore that cock of yours. Why don't you come over here and let me sample it some more?"

"I'd rather sample you."

Ray leaned over the bed and grabbed the waistband of her panties. He was gentle and she was definitely wet, practically on fire with just the suggestion of what he planned. Ray pulled down the back of his pants, and Jesse only had to wonder why for a moment. He'd set his tail free and was curling it along her leg, to her thigh. Ray lifted her feet and placed them on his shoulders. There seemed to be a natural place for them to rest between his wings as his mouth lowered to its goal.

As his tongue began to trace the outer lips of her sex, Jesse was torn between throwing her head back in ecstasy and watching the practically obscene sight of the silver skinned alien between her legs. He teased her for an untenable amount of time before she grabbed his hair, rubbing the tips of his horns in the process.

He moaned and finally pushed forward, finding the button of her pleasure. Jesse tightened her grip and let out a moan of her own. Ray's tongue flicked and twirled against her clit, and as she approached orgasm, she felt his tail pushing into her.

"Fuck me!" It came out louder than she intended, but Ray did as he was bid, thrusting his tail in and out while giving her the tongue lashing of a lifetime. Her hips bucked and she circled and spiraled with the pleasure of it all. When she finally lay still, he lowered her knees from his shoulders and grinned. A flick of his tail reminded her it was still inside her. She held her arms out for him.

"Are you sure you want more of me?"

"You've got me wet enough to take a monster cock. I can handle yours."

"I'm not a monster cock."

"No. You're alien cock. That's different."

"How is that different?"

"Take off your pants and I'll show you."

Ray looked skeptical, but he lowered his pants and let his straining cock free.

Jesse sat up, loving the feel of his tail still inside her as she did. She grabbed his cock with two hands and gave it a little encouragement that it definitely did not need. Ray's breath caught in his throat before he cleared it.

"What is your explanation?"

"I don't have one, I just wanted to get my hands on your cock."

"Naughty." Ray grabbed her hands and pushed her back down to the bed, pinning them above her head. She felt so vulnerable and yet powerful at the same time, knowing that one word would stop him, one word and he would withdraw. She had no intention of uttering that word.

Instead, she ground her hips against his cock. "Put it inside me."

Ray withdrew his tail and slid his cock deep inside her. "Yes, that's it."

"I won't last long if you..."

"Keep begging you to fuck me? Put your alien spunk inside me."

"I want you. I want you forever." He punctuated his sentence with a full thrust and Jesse lost the ability to speak. Everything came out as a shriek or a gasp or a moan. She wrapped her legs tight around his ass and urged him on. He was not gentle, but there was no savagery in his thrusts either. He was demanding and possessive in his claiming, but it was exactly what Jesse craved as he pounded into her and each thrust brought a new wave of pleasure to her entire system.

With one deep thrust, growled out his final release. His face rippled with pleasure, baring all of his fangs. Anyone else would have scared her, but Ray could have bit her right there and she would have encouraged him on. He didn't though. He collapsed in a heap and then rolled off her, nearly off the bed.

"You're not used to sleeping in a bed, are you?" she asked.

"Wings. We don't do well on our backs. We sleep in stone form, not in a bed."

He readjusted so he was on his stomach beside her. He reached his hand out to stroke her still heaving belly.

"I hadn't thought of that before," she admitted.

"Humans don't have to think of things like that."

"I like your wings."

"I like your everything."

Jesse smiled back at him. "So. What did you find?"

"Three bugs. And a camera. He was quite thorough."

"So he probably has pictures of me in the buff?"

"I'd guess so."

"But why me? Why am I so interesting?"

"They're not after you. They're after me. I think they've been watching me for a while. They want to get their hands on my tech, now that they have a better idea of what I can do. You are just a convenient way to get to me."

Jesse sat up. "Did you bring the envelope back?"

"Yes, but-"

She scooted off the bed and sprinted out to the living area in the buff. He'd placed the envelope on a table just inside the door. She grabbed it and headed back into the bedroom. Ray was sitting on a stool by the bed. Now that she considered his wings, all the benches made perfect sense. They allowed him a space to rest his butt, with his wings draped over the side.

He hadn't opened the envelope yet, but by the feel of it, Jesse knew that her fake sigil was inside.

"Let me," Ray said holding out a hand. With his claw, he could easily open the envelope like he was carrying around his own letter opener. She handed it over. "Just in case. I'm immune to most Earth poisons, and I wouldn't put it past Rose to be that devious. Ray poured the contents into his hand. He examined the paper and and her fake. He licked it once.

Jesse stared at him questioningly.

"I think it's okay. This is a very good copy, by the way. The crystal though. That's not fake. That's from a true sigil. Might have been from mine. The Rose had years to disassemble it. It goes to show that they've been trying to recreate it, even though the technology is still way beyond Earth's capabilities.

"Morris Granson," he said, looking at the paper that had come with the device. It was typed neatly on Compass Rose stationary. In the middle of the paper was simply a name and an address. "That's a name I haven't heard in a long time."

"I've never heard it before."

"He was a friend of Olivia. A great while ago."

"A special friend… or a friend friend?"

The look on his face was that of a father who didn't really want to know.

"He had the wrong priorities. He wanted a trophy, not someone who could think for herself."

"And did you unencourage him?"

"I didn't have to. Olivia did it for me."

There was more to the story and Jesse was interested in hearing all the sides. But now she was beginning to understand why the Rose Syndicate had recruited her for the scheme. She had an in. She could say that she'd found something from Morris in her aunt's possessions, and now she wanted to meet him. It would be a good enough excuse.

"Do you fit in an Uber?" she asked, giving him a once over.

"If I have to. Why?"

"Because neither of us own a car, silly."

"Actually…"

"Ray, have you been holding out on me?"

❧ I 2 ❧

FRELINRAY

It had been too damn long since he'd sat behind the wheel of a car. Despite the awkwardness of his wings, Ray had been in love the with automobiles since he'd seen the first Model T's. They were primitive compared to Durassian tech, but so much fun, the freedom to drive. They also now came in tinted windows to hide him from passers by. No one looked twice at a black SUV with tinted windows in New York.

"This is a smooth ride," Jesse said. "How come I've never seen you use it?"

"Never had the reason to." He shrugged. He took a deep breath and inhaled her scent. It was mixed with Olivia's today. She'd borrowed one of Olivia's favorite scarves, dressing the part of a Bohemian great niece to attract the attention of her aunts former amour.

"How far is it to Westchester?" she asked him.

"About twenty minutes without traffic." There was always traffic.

"This is much better than a cab."

"Cabbies tend to freak out when they see a monster in their back seat camera."

He knew from experience. It was better to hoof it most of the time. At least with the toll cameras, he was hidden by the sheer mass of people coming through.

"Really, now. I can't manage to understand why. I also don't understand how you can just let a prime vehicle sit. Doesn't that cost you a relative fortune? The garage space alone."

Ray sighed. True, the top of the line SUV was a luxury, but he needed space for his wings and tall stature. It only took up one spot in the garage, and with the rest of the tenants willing to shell out ridiculous amounts of cash for the privilege having a parking spot, it more than covered his costs for keeping it. But that wasn't why he sighed. He still hadn't fessed up to the whole truth.

"I own the building."

"Which one?"

"Both of them."

"What?!"

"I made some very wise investments in the 1800s. When I came over during the war, you have to remember that the average rent for an apartment was fifty bucks a month. I wanted security and privacy. It just made sense to buy real estate." He shrugged and kept driving. When he glanced back over to her seat, she was ogling at him with a new sense of wonder.

"You're rich," she said finally.

"Yes, I have a very diverse portfolio. Anyone who lived through the Great Depression learned that's the only way to go. Old money is also good at making more money."

"No wonder you weren't interested in my piddly twelve thousand in rent money."

"No. I was more interested in protecting you."

"And boning me?"

"Added perk."

They smiled briefly at each other as he continued to negotiate through the traffic. A short while later, they pulled up in front of a mansion that looked as if it had come straight out of the pages of a Poe story.

"Gothic much?" Jesse quipped.

"Gothic Revival. I could probably perch up there for a while, but it's not like one of those old cathedrals in England where I weathered nearly a century."

"Is it possible he has a gargoyle fetish? Maybe has a few of your buddies in there?"

"Not very likely. Most of them I think stayed local to Europe."

"But if he has a sigil, maybe he knows what it is and is keeping it for someone."

"I don't know if we can take that chance."

Just showing up unannounced on his doorstep had some risks attached, but there was no guarantee that they weren't going to get the door slammed in their face. He had already begun formulating a plan that was little more than an unsophisticated cat burglary in case that happened. However, it would go a lot smoother if he could just lay eyes on its location first. He was hoping Jesse could get them that far at least.

When he broke in, he wanted her as far away as possible. The police would have a hard time prosecuting him for the crime. He had a few dozen places to fly and stone sleep the heat away, but Jesse wanted to keep living and working in the area. Like Olivia, he doubted he could get her to move.

The spark of hope lit him and he tried to squash it down. If things continued to go his way, it was possible the two of them could be together, raise a family, and do all the things his heart had ached to do with Jessenia.

Ray parked them down the street, wanting to keep their presence and vehicle as far from describable as possible. The walk up to the front of the mansion wasn't gated, but there was quite a long drive, long enough for anyone to be alerted and ready for intruders. The front door was a large solid piece of oak, but in the corner, there was a very modern camera mounted. He stayed back, out of view while Jesse rang the bell. No use alarming the man with the view of Ray through the camera.

The door was opened by a young woman with a mane of bleach blond hair in a skirt that was slightly too short and tight for Ray's taste. Her dress was low cut and if he were not mistaken, her breasts were artificially enlarged. She tottered on heels as if she were not at all used to wearing them. Or perhaps she was already drunk at ten o'clock in the morning.

"Are you here to fix the, hic, hot tub?" she asked Jesse.

"Not exactly, but Ray here is very good with machines. I bet he can get it up and running in no time," Jesse said, smooth as glass as she stepped in past the woman. "Is Morris around?"

"Morris is always around. Champagne? I'm not sure you're his type. Maybe you could roll the skirt a little and take off that scarf?"

Ray felt his body tighten with annoyance. This strange woman wanted Jesse to be put on display for another man.

"So, Morris is a lech," Jesse stated calmly as she unwrapped the scarf from around her neck.

"Oh, big time. But don't worry, he's so ancient all he can do is look, so I figure it's a pretty good deal. He'll leave me a bundle and all I have to do is run around in a bikini a few hours a day. It's a real hard life, let me tell you." She laughed and took another swig of the flute of champagne she'd grabbed off the table.

"Got anywhere a girl can freshen up?" Jesse asked. The woman pointed to a bathroom off the main hall and Jesse put her hand on Ray's shoulder. "Well then, why don't you show Ray the hot tub and I'll spruce myself up?"

Ray didn't like splitting up, but the woman seemed harmless enough as she linked his arm and happily escorted him to the room with the hot tub. She seemed too intoxicated to notice that he was taller than he appeared. Either that, or his perception filter was actually doing what it was supposed to do, tricking the silly humans into thinking he was completely harmless and nonthreatening.

The mansion was furnished in a classical style, dripping with antiques and millions in paintings and fine vases. It was a veritable museum with only a few modern improvements. There was a chair lift built into the main staircase and electric outlets cleverly designed to hide into the woodwork. He'd once considered buying a place like this, out in the countryside of England, far away from city life. However, Olivia would have ended up bored to death, and there was no way of insuring that Hitler and his bombs would never intrude.

New York had been the better choice. The hot tub was obviously a more recent addition to the gothic mansion and sat adjacent to an outdoor pool. He opened the filter box and within a few minutes of tinkering, the thing was up and running again.

"You are a miracle worker. Because it's almost time for me to, you know, and I so did not want to get into the water when it was only lukewarm." She put down her flute and suddenly pulled her top off, revealing the barely there bikini top. He tried not to roll his eyes as she shimmied out of her skirt. "So if he asks you if you want to bonk me, the answer is no, mainly because you're just a little old for me, okay? I mean, you're nice and all. I'd suck your cock for fixing the tub, but you know."

Ray did not know. He had no intention of going anywhere near her but thought it more polite to just nod. Jesse appeared and Ray nearly growled. She'd somehow managed to take off her shirt and twist the scarf into a top that was nearly as revealing as the other woman's. Her hair, originally pulled back in a modest bun, now cascaded over her shoulders.

The woman next to him smiled and clapped her hands together.

"You got the idea, girlfriend. Just don't go trying to horn in on my job."

"I'm quite happy with my current employment. But I figured this might soften Morris up."

The woman looked at Ray. "Oh get over yourself, gramps. How long before the hot tub is warm?"

The heater was going at max capacity. "I'd guess an hour. But it's probably warm enough as is. Warmer than the pool, at least."

Jesse raised an eyebrow at him as he watched the woman turn and head into the pool.

"Don't ask," he told her.

She actually chortled.

"I don't think I have the pleasure of knowing the two of you," a voice said from behind them. Ray turned to see a shriveled up version of the man he once knew. His eyes were still clearly on the bleach blonde bouncing slowly into the water.

"I take that back. I think we have met," Morris said. There was that hint of recognition that Ray had learned to identify. It was the sign of someone remembering a form that hadn't aged in fifty years. Morris had aged, way beyond his years. He sat in a motorized wheelchair, blanket covering his lap. His hair was gone and his skin was covered in liver spots. He licked his wrinkled lips as he turned to Jesse.

"I'm here on behalf of my aunt. I believe the two of you were close at one point. Olivia Alves."

His eyes didn't leave Ray. In fact, he squinted harder, but Jesse stepped in front of him and flashed an attractive smile.

"Do you remember Olivia?"

"I do. She was a firecracker. Refused me though. Needed more space, whatever that means."

"She was a free spirit. Never married. Didn't want to get tied down with anything."

"I put two wives under the ground. Both of them thought they'd outlive me and get their hands on my money." Morris cackled.

"Well, I'm not here for your money. I'm here because my aunt mentioned something to me before she died about a special collection that you have. Of artifacts. Ones that certain people at the Rose Syndicate have a hankering for."

"If you're one of those asswipes, you can be on your way, no matter how pretty you are."

Jesse laughed and smiled even brighter. "On the contrary, Morris. It is my plan to do everything within my power to make the Rose Syndicate as miserable as possible. But I need your help to do it," she said. She bent down closer to Morris, giving him a better view of her cleavage.

Morris smiled and smacked the arm of his chair. "You are definitely your aunt's kin. She had a way of being... follow me."

Morris wheeled his chair at a surprisingly fast clip out of the pool area and back into the main house. "I've got quite a collection here. Most of it I can't even appreciate anymore because I'm too short and blind, but I'll be damned if the bastards are going to get their hands on it. Every piece has been categorized and been given a place to go after I'm dead. Five years ago, I finished the list and since then, most of the major museums have been slobbering over me to die."

"Well that's not very polite."

"When you are 97, you get used to it."

He stopped the wheelchair in front of a glass case. On the top was a vase with gargoyles carved into the handles. A second piece was a bit of stained glass that also had some fearful gargoyles being speared by a cross wielding knight.

Ray flashed back through his history. Those had been some horrific and terrible times. They'd only had moments to flee their sinking ship, and many had been burdened with too heavy a load on what turned out to be a long flight to a solid piece of land. They had dropped precious cargo as they'd flown, and some had not made it. They'd vanished below the waves, never to be seen again.

The survivors had made camp on a beach, and a few startled humans had come to ogle at them. Their leader had tried some primitive communication, tried to make peace, but they'd been taken as monsters, as beasts to slay.

His people had scattered after the humans had killed their leader. It was safer to wait and hide out the centuries, hoping for a rescue that might never come.

"St. George and the Dragon," Morris said. "One of the earliest versions, but I think we both know what we're looking at."

Ray stared down at him, but said nothing. He gained nothing by revealing his cards so early in the game.

"What about jewelry? Amulets? Got anything shiny?" Jesse's tone seemed more dumb interest than pointed curiosity.

"Open that drawer over there."

He pointed to one of the drawers under the case. Jesse slid it open and Ray had to stop himself from immediately making a grab for the contents. It was the biggest collection of Durassian tech that he had seen for over a thousand years.

"Many of these have been salvaged from the bottom of the ocean. Most people think they belong to an ancient civilization that was flooded thousands of years ago."

"Is that what you think?" Jesse asked.

"No. I think it's the Rose Syndicate perpetrating a huge hoax on thousands of private collectors. They're creating this whole shit storm so people with buy up their pieces. But you know what? They're worthless, created by a bunch of hacks in the thirties who were desperate for money. And every time they ran out, they just "found" a new piece or two. And because they keep the whole thing hush hush, they can ask outrageous prices for everything."

His whole experience here on this primitive rock had boiled down to how the locals could make a fast fortune by exploiting his tragedy. The worst moments of his life reduced down to a drawer full of trinkets and fakes. He clenched his fists and fought the urge to unfurl his wings and drop every Rose agent he could find off the edge of a very tall cliff.

Jesse seemed to sense his anger and kept her smile plastered in place. "Then why do you have so much of it?"

"Because I've had it for years. I was young and rich and stupid and bought into their whole schtick. I've gotten much wiser in my old age. Besides, art is only worth what someone is willing to pay for it. And when I die, it'll still be worth a fortune, because there are just as many stupid young rich idiots lined up to buy."

His laugh was dry and humorless. It ended with a little rattling cough that signaled to Ray that the man was not long for this world. It was unfortunate that he needed to check the sigil now, and couldn't wait. With all the possibilities in this drawer, even if half of it was fake, Ray could possibly fix his perception filter circuits. He'd no longer be stuck on grumpy old fedora sweater Ray. If he planned a true life with Jesse, he'd need to be able to match her persona. They could move out of the city, buy an estate out in the country where Jesse wouldn't be limited to a studio.

He wanted to ask her, but Morris prevented any side conversations. Jesse was still hunting through the drawer. Her fingers tickled upon the sigil, the true and obvious object that she was interested in.

It lit up when she touched it. His residual DNA on her fingertips was enough for it to sense his presence.

"You see? They can't even be tasteful with their fakes. They have to make it light up. I've checked but I haven't found any wires or circuitry. At least not without destroying the outside of the case.

Jesse picked it up. She circled around to the windows to look at it in the light. The crystal in the center shone a bright sprinkle of red dots across the room as she held it up to the sunlight.

"It's so pretty. Looks a little like that 'Staff of Ra' gizmo from that movie."

Jesse circled back around the cabinet and put it back in the drawer.

"Now, you were saying something about sticking it to the Rose Syndicate," Morris inquired.

"Well, honestly, it would probably cost you a lot of money, and I wouldn't want to do that to such a good friend of my aunt."

"Child, I have more money than I can spend before I die."

"If you give us the contents of that drawer, we can make sure the Rose Syndicate is blown wide open," Ray said quietly. "Everything they've been working for over the past century will lead to jack shit."

"And how do I know I can trust you?" Morris said, looking up at him with a critical eye.

"As you said, what do you have to lose?" Jesse said. "At worst, we take some fakes off your hands. At best, you get sweet, sweet revenge on the assholes that cheated and scammed you." She leaned down toward Morris. His eyes once again undressing her as he stared down her cleavage. "I'm personally invested in this since one of those bastards tried to kill me. Threw me off a roof." Jesse realized a moment after she spoke that it might lead to unanswerable questions. "Tried to, anyway," she added. "Do you know why? Because I refused to cheat someone. Refused to cheat you, as it turns out."

"Bunny!"

The blonde came bouncing to the room. She must have toweled off, but was still wearing the barely there bikini.

"Get these nice people a crate. And you sweetie," he said to Jesse. "Why don't you have some champagne? I think your friend over there got the hot tub working again."

"I'll take some champagne, but we're kind of on a tight schedule."

Morris wheeled off with Jesse to the other room, leaving

Bunny and Ray to pack up the drawer. Bunny did so with surprising care for a poolside eye candy.

"Don't look so surprised. I have a degree in archaeology. This is only a side job for a gap year. And before you get into it, yeah, I know. But it pays the bills. More than pays the bills."

Ray shrugged as he helped put the artifacts into the crate. He had a moment of panic when touched the sigil and it did not react. He realized then that Jesse had already switched it out. She must have done so when she'd examined it the first time. Smart and smooth, that's what she was. Just in case Morris changed his mind, they'd still have what they want.

He picked up the crate and handed Bunny a card with his number. "You ever need a real job, or if he collects any more of these artifacts, give me a call. I can probably give you a hand."

Bunny looked skeptical, but she took the card and stuffed it in her bikini.

Jesse was laughing way too loud and patting Morris on the shoulder when he came out into the lobby carrying the crate. She put down her champagne flute and smiled down at him.

"Thank you so much, Morris. I can't wait to make that horrid man pay for what he tried to do to me."

She winked at him and then walked out the door. Moments later, they were back in the car and on the road.

"That creepy old man tried to get up my skirt three times in five minutes!"

Ray wanted to tell her that she deserved it for wearing such a skimpy outfit, but he knew that had been the best way to butter up Morris. Fending off the hands of a wheelchair bound geezer was nothing compared to keeping The Rose Syndicate at bay after they learned Jesse had been successful in getting multiple objects from Morris. His stomach churned with the thought.

"We don't have to go back to New York. We could go some-where else," Ray began.

"The Rose Syndicate will find us. Facial recognition soft-ware and all that jazz."

"Giles can help with that. With this tech, I might be able to fix my perception filter."

"You mean you won't be stuck in a sweater vest for the rest of your life?"

"Exactly."

"I dunno. I kinda think the fedora is sexy."

"It won't work on you any more. You've seen and… touched too much for your brain to process me any differently than what it does now."

"So I should buy you a real fedora."

"I probably have one around somewhere. A trenchcoat too, although that look went out of style sometime after I came to New York."

"I like you just the way you are, sweater vest and all."

Ray beamed. "That's the champagne talking."

"I had like three sips, silly."

"You're a lightweight. One drink and you're demanding a dance."

"That's because I wanted a dance, not because I had anything to drink."

Ray smirked and pulled up the hem of her skirt on one side.

"What are you doing?"

"Checking to see if you think I'm a lecherous old man."

"Of course, I think you're a lecherous old man. But you're my lecherous old man.".

JESSE

Jesse tried to get rid of that pit in the bottom of her stomach as she locked both deadbolts on her apartment. She knew that the elevator was now limited to the floor below and Ray had installed a serious set of electronic locks on the stairway door. The only way someone was getting up here was with his permission.

Maybe some tea would calm her nerves. And some comfort food. Jesse started some hot water as Ray headed to his apartment with the box of goodies.

It totally felt like a ramen day. Quick hot noodles with enough sodium to kill a horse. She stopped for a moment and tried to think. Had she even seen Ray eat? What did he eat? He was an alien. For all she knew, he could be completely allergic to noodles. Or maybe he was a vegan.

She left the water in the kettle and circled around to Ray's apartment. He was sitting on a stool next to a workbench by the crate. He was pulling out each item and examining it like a kid at Christmas who had too many presents and didn't know where to start. She came up behind him and peered over his shoulder.

"Morris was right. A lot of these are fakes. The question is, how many of them were built from models that the Rose Syndicate still owns?"

"I think it might be on the dangerous side to poke the bear again," Jesse said. "I'm going to fix myself some noodles."

He nodded, thoroughly engrossed in a little silver black square.

"And some tea."

"Right."

"Do you want some? I mean, you're an alien. I don't even know what you eat."

"Not as much as a human, but I can eat human food. I supplement it with other things."

"Things."

"I may have been snacking on your tile."

"Seriously?"

"It's a helluva lot cheaper than the dumping fees in New York." Jesse crossed her arm.

"Well, would you like a side of noodles with my bathtub?"

"Yes, please. Salty is great for my diet."

Jesse rolled her eyes and headed back to her apartment. The water was ready so she made two noodle cups and two cups of tea.

When she got back to Ray's apartment, carrying the four mugs, he had the sigil in his hands. It was glowing brightly, brighter than when she had put it up to the window. The entire apartment was bathed in an eerie red light.

"They're here."

"Oh that's not ominous at all," Jesse said. "I thought you checked for bugs."

"No, not them. My people, they are actually coming. We're being rescued." Her chest tightened. Jesse bit her lip to stop from panicking. If Ray left her, Pablo would find her for sure, with or without Giles help. She'd have nowhere to go. As secure as this apartment might be, there were no guarantees about what would happen if she stepped out the front door unprotected.

"Why did it take them this long?"

"Temporal mechanics is my guess. The message isn't any more than a pick up point and date and time."

"You mean they can't just beam me up Scottie, any time they want?"

"No. It's complicated, but they have to find the least likely time for detection, and with the angles, certain pick up points make sense." Ray put the sigil down on the table.

He sighed heavily and turned toward Jesse. She didn't exactly like that sigh. Ray looked sad and a bit forlorn. She doubted noodles and tea would make that sigh go away. But she knew something that might.

"C'mere." Jesse grabbed his arm and led him into his bathroom. "Help me with this, would you?" she said, turning around and lifting her hair. She was perfectly capable of undoing the knot in the scarf by herself, but she reveled in the intimacy of having Ray slowly untie and unwrap the scarf from her body. Once the scarf dropped to the floor, he took his time feeling the weight of her breasts in his hands before taunting each nipple into a puckered tip. Jesse guided his hands down to the buttons on her skirt. He managed those too, slipping the skirt past her hips, taking her panties with it.

Ray's fingers followed it down, and traced her pussy lips on the way back up.

"Don't you want to turn on the water?" Jesse asked as he teased her folds again.

"It's voice activated. Computer? Shower on, setting three."

Sure enough, water began to pour from the many spouts. Ray decided to amuse himself until the water heated by pushing his finger further inside her. She was already wet and waiting for him. He urged her forward once the water began to steam.

"What about your pants? Shorts. Won't they get wet?"

"They can take the water."

She pulled at his shorts. "I mean your tail. Surely you want to wash your tail?"

Ray laughed and nibbled on her ear.

"Oh, my tail, eh? You want my tail?"

"Only if you want to give it to me," Jesse said with a smile. Ray was not smiling. He was removing his shorts. He picked her up and a few short steps later, they were being pelted with heated rain from all sides. Ray pushed her up against one of the walls. It should have been cold, but it wasn't. Not that she was feeling anything but a searing heat right now as he took his tail and thrust it inside her. His finger went back to her clit and her world was on fire.

"You like that? You like being fucked like this," he said, giving his tail an extra flex for emphasis.

"I like your cock too." Jesse illustrated her point by reaching for it, wrapping two hands around his shaft and stroking them up and down his hard length. Ray began to thrust his hips in time with the talented tail. She loved the feel of him sliding through her hands. The tired, worried look on his face was definitely gone, but she had a way to push it one step further. She bent down and put out her tongue, tasting the tip of his cock as he pressed through her fingers. Ray definitely seemed to enjoy it. He moaned and continued as if his cock were striving to reach her mouth but was just a fraction of an inch too far away.

Feeling her own pleasure rising, ready to fracture her, Jesse gave in to the game she'd always planned to lose and took the head of his cock into her mouth. She teased him mercilessly with her tongue, lashing it along the head and running the length of his slit.

"Oh! I'm not, I can't-"

"Give it to me!" Jesse demanded. Ray thrust harder with his tail and Jesse nearly fell over with the pleasure as she came. Ray grabbed her head, steadying her before one final thrust with his cock. He shouted his cry to the heavens and Jesse pulled back just enough to watch the long ropes of cum splurt out, covering her chin and breasts.

Jesse was sad that it was already beginning to wash away. She rather liked being covered in alien spunk. It wasn't like her to have such dirty thoughts but for some reason, Ray brought it out in her, like they were meant to be. Reality came crashing down on her. She stood up and Ray wrapped his arms around her, then enveloped the two in his wings.

"How long do we have?" she asked him.

"The end of October. Strangely enough, the one night that I can walk out in the open and no one gives a shit."

"Halloween."

"Yeah."

"It's my favorite holiday."

"Mine too."

"You know, if we stand here like this, I'm never going to get your cum washed off of me."

Ray laughed, heartily. "True, but I do believe you've not given me back my tail." He wiggled it inside her to illustrate his point. His fingers trailed back down to her clit. He kneeled, balancing her on his thigh. A few more seconds later and she was grabbing at him, trying to get a purchase of something while she came again. He let her calm down a bit before lifting her onto his cock.

Ray was in no hurry this time, and apparently had no concern for running out of hot water. He worked her through her paces until she was practically limp with pleasure. Only then did his urgency increase as he chased his second orgasm. Jesse held on to him, expecting his arms to come around her tighter, for his hips to make one last thrust before spilling himself deep inside her.

Instead she found herself on the floor of the shower looking up a her gargoyle towering above her in all his glory. He spread his wings wide, and gave her a mischievous grin. Jesse felt elated in her vulnerability, knowing she was safe and protected and yet still at the mercy of her alien lover. Ray took his throbbing cock into his hand, and with a few strokes threw back his head and covered her breasts with ropes of his cum.

"Now you are truly messy," Ray said, still gloating from above her.

"You want me to complain?" Jesse smeared his spunk around on her breasts. He folded his wings again, allowing the water to fall on her once more.

"Never, my sweet."

He pulled her up and gave her a thorough rinse before carrying her out of the shower. Now a nap was definitely in order. Getting messy was a tiring exercise.

❧ 14 ❧

FRELINRAY

"Eureka!" Ray shouted loudly as he lifted his head from the workbench. Jesse sat straight up on the couch and he felt bad for a moment. She had been sleeping and he hadn't even noticed.

"I fixed it! I can be anyone I want to be now."

"Ooh, how about Harrison Ford. Not old Harrison, but like vintage 1980 where he was both Han Solo and Indiana Jones?"

"It works better if I'm non descript. Not ugly, not handsome. You know, just another guy walking down the street."

"Shame."

"It means that I…"

He didn't finish that thought out loud. Something deep within him was torn. He had a duty, and if the war still raged after a thousand years, he was sworn to defend his people to the end. Or to stay here and live out his days with Jesse.

So many of his fellow Khargals had chosen that option. They'd closed the hope of ever being rescued and gone on to live their lives. He had waited and waited. Finally he was being rewarded for that faith, except now, he had Jesse.

He could take her with him, into space, into a potential war zone. Once he was aboard, he could use his skills and the new techniques he'd developed to barter a new position. Ray could take the pair of them away.

Or he could ignore the call, stay here with Jesse and spend the rest of his life on the run from the Rose Syndicate. If he'd learned one thing throughout the years, it was that no matter what form it took, there was always some group trying to take away what was his.

"What does it mean?" Jesse prompted. She approached and leaned against him. He loved the weight and heat of her body against him.

"It means I won't have to find that fedora and get it out of mothballs."

"Oh, I still think you need to find that fedora."

Jesse actually bit him on the back of his shoulder and he let out a growl of pleasure. She squeaked and ran. Shortly, they were playing a game of hide and seek that she desperately wanted to lose.

An hour later, Ray was back on task. Ray translated the coordinates and found the spot. "I have the coordinates. It looks like there's good news and bad news."

"Hit me."

"It's definitely isolated. Out in the middle of Canada."

"Is that the good news or the bad news?"

"The good. The bad is it's on the other side of Canada. It's a 3000 mile trip from here."

"Road Trip?"

"No. I'll talk to Giles and see if I can get a chartered flight."

"Canadian wilderness," Jesse said, looking at the dot on the map. "That should be simple. If you have to go."

"Jesse."

"No, I get it. You're the oddball out. The fish out of water. Hell, people here have tried to kill you. It only makes sense that you'd want to go back home."

"It's not that I don't want to stay. I have a duty. I'm a soldier at heart, and I made a commitment to my people."

"I think a thousand years marooned on an alien planet counts as fulfilling your commitment." Jesse stood up and walked out onto the garden patio. The air was slightly chilly for her sensitive skin. He wanted to wrap her and keep her safe for a millenium.

"There are no guarantees, but I might be able to take you with me," he offered.

"What?"

"If you were my mate, they couldn't reasonably request that I separate from you. I don't know what the conditions will be like, and Duras is not a hospitable location for a human. But there are other resource ships, there must still be, and life on them could be quite pleasant."

Ray stumbled over his words as she turned around, her eyes wide.

"You mean you want me to come up to your spaceship? Leave everything I know behind and take a chance on an alien world?"

"It was just a suggestion. You don't have to. I mean I'll have plenty of money for you to live wherever you like. You could go someplace tropical. South America? The Caribbean?"

"Stop. Stop right there. I've been stressing out about you disappearing off the face of the Earth and now you say that I can come with you? How long have you been considering this?"

"Since I first knew I had to leave."

"You big stone idiot. I'm definitely coming with you. Screw the Caribbean. I hear crime there is skyrocketing and there's a hurricane every other year. And South America is full of Nazis."

Ray didn't let her continue. He wrapped her even tighter and brought her mouth to his for a searing kiss. She melted like butter in his arms. When he broke off the kiss, he knelt next to her.

"Then we shall have to mate."

"So what have we been doing this whole time?"

"Having fun?"

She gave him a little punch on the arm.

"For a Khargal to mate, he must transfer his mating fluid into the bloodstream of his female. It allows for the match to be fertile, among other things."

"Ah, so premarriage birth control."

"The mating with another species can sometime have other side effects."

"Like what?"

"It can extend your life quite a lot."

"That's sounds good."

"But it can also change your skin tone and texture, allow you to see better in the dark, awaken some of your extrasensory perceptions."

"So there's no telling what voodoo I might end up with."

"Precisely. It is not a commitment to take lightly. It is until death do us part."

Jesse took a deep breath.

"Ray-" she began. A ringtone rang out in the distance. It was his phone. He only gave it out to a few people. "You should get that."

He didn't recognize the number, but he answered it anyway.

"Yo. Ray? Jesse there? She ain't pickin' up," Luis said from the other end of the line.

"Pablo's back. My boy Sam says he and some of his guys were messing with an SUV in the next building over."

"Keep away from them. Jesse's here and safe. Pablo's pissed off and probably looking for someone to take it out on."

"I tased him!" Jesse yelled out from behind Ray.

Ray could hear Luis laughing as he hung up the phone.

"The car might be compromised."

"I gathered that. What kind of flight are we going to need to take? Surely we can just head to the airport and go from there.

Clearly, money is no issue if we're abandoning the planet. Do you have another plan of how you are going to divide your wealth up?"

Ray stopped to think. He didn't need the money anymore. He needed time and breathing space to make plans. Were there any resources here on Earth that he needed to take with him? Even though they'd had a thousand years, Earth tech had not caught up with his world. Was he going to be any use at all when they returned, or will have all the technology outpaced him as well? He pushed that thought aside.

"I think we can leave some for Luis and his block. I could leave him the whole building. Also Giles, so they can keep the Rose Syndicate in check. I'll make an appointment with my lawyer."

"You have a lawyer?"

"Of course I do."

"Can we do something about Pablo before we leave?"

"Want me to snap his neck?"

"I... no. Maybe frame him for some crime so he ends up in jail where that sociopath belongs. Or maybe just set fire to all his pastel suits."

Good. He was hoping Jesse would never be that bloodthirsty.

"Speaking of belongings, there's no guarantee you'll be able to take anything with you. It might just be you, me and a beam."

"What makes you think I need anything else?"

He loved the way that she smiled up at him.

Ray heard it this time, Jesse's phone ringing from her apartment.

"That's probably Luis again. He won't be satisfied until you talk to him personally."

Jesse hopped up and headed over to her apartment. Ray headed to his computer to set up some of the plans he needed to make in the week and half before Halloween. It wasn't exactly easy these days to charter an international flight into an airfield mostly reserved for mining traffic. That seemed to be the closest point to anywhere near the coordinates. What he hadn't laid out to Jesse was the third coordinate. They'd have to be up high enough to be swept up in the transfer beam.

Jesse came sprinting back with a look of concern in her face. "That wasn't Luis. It was Pablo on Luis's phone."

15

JESSE

"What does he want?" There was a cold chill in Ray's voice.

All the excitement about their future adventure was seeping out through the cracks.

"He wants the sigil."

"We can't give him the sigil."

"I know, but we can't leave Luis out to dry."

"The last time you tried to make a deal with Pablo, he threw you off a roof. What makes you think he's going to do any better this time?"

"I know!" Jesse started pacing. The panic was creeping up in her gut. "You told Luis to stay out of the way. Why the hell didn't he stay out of the way?"

"Because he's a man. And he was probably trying to impress you. How much time do we have?"

"He wants us to come down in the elevator."

"I'll go down."

"He's expecting me. Alone."

"I've got wings. I can fly."

"And who's to say he won't start shooting the second he sees you? No, it would be better if you hid around the corner or something and I tried to find out where Luis is, so you can rescue him." It wasn't much of a plan, but it was the best she could come up with at this late notice.

"I'm not putting you in the line of fire!"

"I'm putting myself there!"

Ray wrapped himself around her wings and all. She suddenly realized that if he turned to stone, she'd have no way of actually going down the elevator. She'd be caught in a stone embrace until he decided she was out of danger.

"Fine. I've got another idea. It's riskier for Luis, but it might work. You said your perception thingy was fixed?"

"Yeah."

"Could you be me?"

"Possibly, but I don't have a voice modulator. I'd sound just like me."

"Fly me down around the back side of the building, and then you go down the elevator as me. Then you hand over the fake and I peek around to make sure everything's kosher."

"And what are you going to do if it's not?"

"Run like hell?"

"This is not a good plan."

"It's perfectly sound for a five minute plan."

"And what about my voice?"

"Whisper. Tell him you lost it screaming out your orgasms."

Ray chuffed at that, but it at least got him smiling.

"And what if he catches the fake right away?"

"Tell him a yarn. It only works when Ray touches it, or he figured out that the coordinates lead to somewhere in South America. Yeah, send them on a wild goose chase to Brazil. That's good."

"This is not a good plan."

"The other plan involves me in that elevator."

"How about you not going down at all?"

"You need back up. Besides, I can go to the bodega and get help. That way it'll be a few of us against Pablo. I have a feeling there's an advantage to having more eyes around Pablo. He'll be less likely to do something stupid."

"You'll go straight to the bodega."

"Promise."

Ray touched a few buttons on his gizmo and then flew her down the back alley. Ray hopped up a few stories and went into the building through the fire escape. It made sense. If Pablo was haunting the elevator, hoping for a ride up to the roof for another chance to throw her off, he'd be in for a disappointment when he called down from the third floor.

Jesse took off in a sprint, suddenly wishing she'd taken the time to put on more comfortable shoes. Her little ballet flats that she wore around the apartment were fine for lounging, but running in them was a challenge. As a habit, Jesse did not run much at all if she could avoid it.

In through the back of the bodega, she skidded to a halt when she saw Luis behind the counter, just as cool as a cucumber.

"Shit, Luis, where's your phone?"

"Jesse-" He paused when a pat of his pockets came up empty.

"Where the fuck is my phone?"

"Pablo has it. Said you were kidnapped."

Jesse didn't understand the entire stream of Spanish that came out of his mouth, but she was sure most of it was naughty. "Fuckin' Puta!"

"Ray went to go meet him. To do an exchange. We've got to warn him that you're okay."

Jesse dialed Ray's number. No one picked up. She decided to change tactics. She called 911 and gave them her apartment address.

"Oh, my God. There's like this creepy Mexican guy standing in the lobby of my apartment. I think he's just pushing random call buttons to see if someone will buzz him in. I'm pretty sure he's got a gun. I think he sees me."

She hung up the phone.

Luis stared at her. "I'm not Mexican."

"I know that. I was talking about Pablo, even though I'm pretty sure he's not Mexican either. I'm hoping playing dumb white blonde will decrease their response time."

"That's cold, man."

"Desperate times, desperate measures," Jesse shrugged.

Jesse didn't hear any sirens, but hopefully, that was because they were going with the silent approach. Maybe bringing a SWAT team. Probably not, but she could hope.

Luis was fingering his baseball bat.

"You shouldn't get involved."

"He stole my phone! And used it to commit a felony."

"I'll see what I can do about getting it back."

Jesse ran out the door before Luis could convince her otherwise.

She hadn't gone more than twenty feet before she spotted Pablo waiting on the street outside her apartment. Ray was nowhere in sight.

"Did you think that would work?" Pablo called. "We've had years to develop ways of subduing… him." He said, looking around as if the muggles would catch on that they were talking about an alien.

"Where is he?"

"Safe and sound until you give us what we want."

"What do you want?"

"The real beacon."

"Well, good luck with that, because Mr. Wingman put it somewhere out of reach of anyone without wings."

"Where exactly?"

"I don't know. He flew off and stashed it in some hidey hole."

Pablo squinted, apparently buying her story.

"Then I have no further need for you."

Despite there being a large number of people out and about, Jesse got the impression that Pablo didn't care. He was going to shoot her in broad daylight as if he were immune to any and all prosecution.

There was nowhere to hide, just hope that Pablo was a horrible shot. But then something miraculous happened. The police actually arrived. Someone in the crowd yelled, "He's got a gun!" People scrambled out of sight and Jesse took that moment to duck behind a car. When she next looked, Pablo was screaming like a stuck pig and there was a cop kneeling on his back.

Jesse turned and headed back to the bodega. Luis was not there. He had probably been the one to get the crowd moving, now that she thought of it.

But where was Ray?

16

FRELINRAY

"**G**o, go, go!" Ray heard the men shout. He was groggy, but in stone sleep, he could still manage to listen in on snatches of the conversation. He got the gist that Pablo was not coming with them.

"He thinks he's so slick."

"Careful. You know how he bugs everything."

"You saw it, he was getting put in handcuffs."

"He'll be out in less than an hour. I'm sure he'll meet us at the rendezvous point."

He muddled out the fact that there was one male and one female voice.

Whatever Pablo had shot him full of was potent stuff, forcing him into an immediate stone sleep. They'd been lucky enough to drag him the few steps out to the van before he'd fully turned. Otherwise, he would have been nearly immoveable without assistance from a trolley.

The driver and her passenger went silent but Ray drifted into consciousness long enough to know they were leaving the city, and heading into a more sparsely populated area.

Jesse. She was unprotected, and Luis was nowhere to be

seen. Ray hadn't wanted to tell Jesse that he was probably already dead. Pablo would have no problem taking his cell phone off his body and leaving it in a dumpster somewhere.

He hoped she had the sense to go see Giles. He was the last hope of getting her safely away from the Syndicate and hopefully getting her and the sigil to the Northwest Territory. He should have mated with her. He should have followed his instincts and filled her with the fluid that had been aching in his glands for weeks now.

It was too late for that now. The last time he had been taken by the Rose Syndicate, it had taken six months for him to escape, and by that time Jessenia had been dead.

No, it wouldn't take him that long, no matter what deal he had to strike with those bastards. He'd be out and away and then he and Jesse could leave this world behind.

They slowed and the van drove down a ramp and underground. There was a jerk, and he felt an elevator in motion. Great. He was in a secret underground base miles from nowhere. Things were getting better and better.

He felt himself being lifted, fought against the stone sleep but was unsuccessful. He was a prisoner in his own body. The sheer effort alone drifted him back out of consciousness.

When he awoke, whatever Pablo had fired into him had left his system. He was in a cell, and Rose had definitely gone a lot more high tech than his last imprisonment. Last time, he'd been tethered with solid iron chains. This time, there was a large clear pane and a room of about a six feet cube. Cameras watched him from every angle.

Pablo stood waiting, looking at his watch.

"You see, we have it down to a science, this new formula. Although we had to estimate your weight compared to our other subjects," hesaid calmly. His normal jacket was missing. Instead, he wore only a light yellow vest with a purple shirt and a pink tie.

"Where's Jesse?"

"Where's our little device? You know the one you stole for us?"

"I didn't steal it. He gave it to me. Ask him yourself."

"That doesn't answer my question."

"Only if you answer my question. Why do you choose to dress as if Easter threw up all over you? You know, it's just not pretty. I mean maybe if your face wasn't so ugly and you didn't look like an egg."

Pablo squinted at him. Ray wanted to get him angry, to not think and open the door. That's where he was probably going to find a flaw in this system, by exploiting human weaknesses and other ego maniacal tendencies.

"Where is it?"

"Carrot and stick? Surely, you're smart enough to know you're going to need leverage over me. That's the only way that I'm going to even think about giving you what you want."

"You see Jesse when you tell me where it is."

"No, I see Jesse now, or you can pry the information from my cold dead brain pan. I'm pretty sure you haven't developed that technology yet."

Pablo's eye twitched and he crossed his arms over his chest. It was a defensive move, and Ray clocked it just as he was busy eyeballing the cameras, the lighting fixtures and perhaps even the glue that held the window in place.

"She's someplace cold and with a limited supply of air, so I'd suggest you hurry."

Ray pressed down his moment of panic. He had no reason to believe that they had her, and Pablo was such a sadist, he'd have no problem putting her on the phone, crying and screaming if he did. Forcing him to listen to Jesse was just up Pablo's alley.

"I don't believe you. I think you're a fat little pastel liar, and until you prove me wrong, I have nothing more to say to you." Ray shrugged, extended both his middle fingers and went into stone sleep. Let the asshole come and try to break off his fingers. He'd smash his head in so fast, he wouldn't know what hit him. From the way Pablo smacked the button on the wall outside his cell, darkening the window, Ray was satisfied that Jesse was out of Pablo's hands, at least for now.

❧ 17 ❧

JESSE

"Contrary to popular belief, I am not the be all and end all of information on the Rose Syndicate. I do what I can, but I have no idea where they took him. I like him. Ray's a great guy, but I don't even know where to look or who to ask."

Jesse had been waiting nearly two hours at Evensong, hoping that her favorite bartender had some answers. Giles, apparently, did not.

"How about his lawyer? Do you know who that is? He said he was going to call him and then all this went crazy."

"That I can help you with. Give me a minute."

Giles ducked back into a room behind the bar and a minute later came out holding a card. "I can't guarantee how much this guy knows, but I'm pretty sure Ray trusts him."

Jesse took the card and looked at the classic font and fine paper stock. The name caught her attention at once: The Law Firm of Lark and Morales. "I think I know why. My mom's maiden name is Lark."

Finding the offices had been easy. Making herself presentable without going back to her apartment had been another story. Instinctively, Jesse knew she should not be using a credit card for anything. It was easily traceable, but she had very little in the bank to start with. At least she didn't have to worry about paying rent, Jesse told herself. She withdrew the last $150 from her account, found a reasonable dress and grabbed some hair ties at a dollar store. A few minutes in a coffee stop restroom and she was at least presentable enough to make it past whatever secretaries were guarding the lawyers' inner sanctum. Another twenty bucks and she had purchased a genuine "Couch" purse from a rather shady street vendor.

When Jesse came out of the elevator and approached the receptionist, the gaze she got was questioning, but barely passing muster. She was an older lady, probably sent out to discourage those who would not be able to pay the retainer of such a ritzy firm.

"Can I help you?" Jesse took on the persona of a woman who'd been kept waiting for a lunch date.

"I'm here to see Mr. Lark."

"Do you have an appointment?"

"I thought so. Jessenia," she said pointedly, trying to get a gaze of the receptionist's screen. "Jessenia Lark." It was a little white lie. In fact, her mother had considered going back to Lark numerous times, but the whole process had become more cumbersome after 9/11. The feds didn't make it easy to change your name anymore. Jesse got the opinion it was just something her mother liked to complain about, rather than take action. One more thing to blame on her no good father and her family that disowned her when she got married.

She'd never met her uncle. Honestly, Jesse had forgotten he existed until she'd seen the card. Her mother never talked about him. Aunt Olivia hadn't either, probably out of deference to her mother. Free child care or not, if she'd known Olivia was fostering a relationship with her scorning brother, she would have had a fit. She knew he didn't approve of her mother's marriage, and when her grandmother had gotten sick, there'd been even more bad blood, but Jessenia had been too young to remember any of it. She figured her uncle would be in his sixties by now. Hopefully, he'd be willing to hear her out and at least start some sort of relationship.

"I'm his niece." Jessenia added.

The receptionist pushed a button and picked up a phone.

"Your, uh, niece is here for a visit?" She paused, shrugged and stood, hanging up the phone. "Right this way."

Jesse followed her past the glass doors and down the hall to a corner office. The receptionist opened the door and ushered her in. Jesse stood there a moment and admired the view. It was one of those offices with a view of most of Manhattan, breathtaking and the mark of someone who's truly made it. The chair was swiveled toward the window, and when it turned slowly around, Jesse frowned at the man in the chair. He couldn't be more than thirty. He was chubby with ruffled dark brown hair. He wasn't wearing a tie and his button down shirt was off by one button.

"Thanks, Helen." The receptionist seemed hesitant to leave, but he waved her off and she went, closing the door behind her.

"You're not my uncle."

"And since my sister doesn't have any kids, you sure as hell aren't my niece." He sighed and looked her over. "You know, I'm not really in the mood for this. Do you know what it's like to have newborn twins?"

"Congratulations?"

"No sleep. I actually abandoned my wife this morning and pleaded that I had to come into the office, just so I could take a nap. And you, whatever your name is, have just disturbed my hard earned, desperately needed sleep."

"Your shirt's buttoned up wrong."

He looked down to verify, but didn't seem to be in a hurry to fix it. "Great. Now, who the hell are you and what do you want?"

"Honestly, I thought you were my uncle."

"How much money do you want? Though honestly, I'm pretty sure I've only got a twenty in my wallet at the moment."

"I don't want your money. I want your help. I'm- My friend, who I think is your client, at least that's what I've been told, is in trouble."

"What's the bail?"

"No, not that kind of trouble. He's been kidnapped, by an evil fat man named Pablo."

"Have you taken your meds?"

"I know, but I really haven't got time to get into the really crazy part, but Giles said Ray trusts you."

Lark nearly fell out of his chair. "Wait, which Ray?"

"Ray... Ray. Fedora? Sweater vest?"

"Fangs?"

Jesse breathed a sigh of relief. "Yes. That one."

"Well, he's not a client. He's family. Wait. You're Jessenia," he said, making a connection.

"Yes."

"Oh, well, then, we're cousins. Thomas Lark, my dad, died a year ago. I'm Tommy. I took over as Ray's lawyer then. What do you mean kidnapped?"

Jesse rambled out the whole story as her cousin righted the buttons on his shirt. He pushed the pager button on the phone. "Helen, I'm going to need a gallon of coffee."

❧

"So you have a week and a half to get Ray and his doohickey to BF Canada to catch a ride on a spaceship, do I have that right?"

"Yes."

"And how can I help?"

"I don't know exactly, but I do know that Ray wanted to settle his affairs before leaving. He was talking about leaving one of the buildings to Luis, whose uncle runs the bodega on the corner, and some money for Giles who works at Evensong. Probably some for you, too, but he got taken before I could figure it out."

"He basically planned to outlive us all, so he doesn't have a will, but I do have some power of attorney to take care of his affairs if need be. I can get an investigator to look into this Pablo and see what we can find out."

Jesse sighed in relief. "Thank you."

Helen came in with some coffee. Tommy practically inhaled it.

"If you don't mind me saying so, cos, you're looking a little worse for wear. There's a couch over there. Why don't you take a little nap while I see what I can put in motion?"

Jesse nodded and went to the couch in question. Despite the worry in her stomach, she drifted off nearly the moment her head hit the armrest.

◈

"**J**esse looks so peaceful on that couch. I'd hate to disturb her." She knew that voice and jack knifed straight off the couch when she heard it. Pablo, in yet another suit stood there, calm as you please, next to Tommy.

"She was talking crazy. Said something about an alien. Rambling about you trying to kill her."

"Don't worry, don't worry. She's just a little crazy, but we give her meds, and all will be right with the world." Pablo had two little pills in his hand.

"Ah, well, I'm not sure I can be a party to forcing her to take any medication that she doesn't want to take."

"No way in fucking hell am I taking anything from Pablo. Did I tell you he confessed to killing his wife? That was right before he tried to kill me the first time," Jesse spat out.

Tommy backed toward the door. For a moment, she could swear he winked at her before exiting.

"Now, now, don't be a little shit," Pablo said through his teeth.

"You're going to have to kill me before I take whatever the hell that is. And you're going to have an awfully difficult way of explaining yourself if you do."

"Why should you be worried about that? You'll be dead. But I don't want you dead anymore. Not yet anyway. Your stubborn fuck buddy is refusing to talk."

"Where is he?" Jesse scrambled off the couch, but she was in the corner, and Pablo was slowly inching forward.

"Take the pills and I'll take you right to him. I promise. Swear even." He couldn't even hide his annoyance any more.

"So you can use me as leverage? Ha. You tried to lie to him, didn't you? And now you need me so he'll talk? But I know too much. As soon as you get what you want, I'll be expendable again. Just like on the street when you were going to shoot me the second time."

"I only tried to shoot you once. The first time I threw you off the roof. Next time, I think nice and personal, you know, close like a knife sliding across your throat. Letting your blood squirt through my fingers." He seemed positively gleeful at the the thought. "Now swallow the fucking pills. They'll make all your troubles go away."

Jesse wondered if screaming bloody murder would do her any good. No, she decided to settle for a swift kick to the balls. Pablo was not ready or fast enough to counter her attack. She got him squarely in his pastel crotch. He bent over in pain and Jesse sprinted for the door.

It was opened by another woman sporting a pantsuit covered

by a blue windbreaker and rather familiar eyes. She circled around Jesse and straight to Pablo.

"Pablo, you're under arrest for threatening a federal witness, and well, everything else. Get up."

Pablo only managed a squeak. The woman handcuffed him anyway. A matching pair of federal agents in US Marshal jackets picked him up by the arms and escorted him out. Tommy came back into his office behind him. He was smiling broadly at the woman.

"Jessenia, meet your other cousin, Margaret Lark."

"Named after our grandmother," Jesse said, finally catching on.

"Yeah, but don't call me Midge."

"Wouldn't dream of it. The last time he was arrested, he had a gun on the streets of New York City and was out in an hour."

"Oh, don't worry. I plan to follow him around and lose his paperwork for a good long time. In fact, his papers might just get misfiled permanently. And welcome to the family, by the way, even though it sounds like you're not long for this world."

Margaret shook her hand and departed, punching her brother on the shoulder. "You owe me one," she called out as she left.

"But what about Ray? How are we going to find him?" Jesse pleaded.

"Oh that's easy. That arrogant son of bitch took a helicopter here. And once threatened with arrest, the pilot was more than happy to share his flight plan and his boss's itinerary. He's even willing to give us a flight back."

"Us?"

"Hell, how else am I supposed to get to know my cousin before she takes a trip off planet? At least that's what I told my wife. I swear, I do not feel guilty. I do not feel guilty."

An hour later and she was airborne, on her way to a field in Pennsylvania.

❧ 18 ❧

FRELINRAY

There was something definitely going on. Ray had lost track of how long he'd been kept in the white room. The lights started to flicker and the circuit that fogged the window had blown and cleared the glass. Ray roused himself from stone sleep to look out at the hallway beyond. There wasn't much to see. He was pretty sure there was a row of cells similar to his. A man sprinted down the hallway as if his life depended on it. There was gunfire a few rooms away, and then ominously, it stopped.

A form entered the far side door, and as it grew closer, Ray thought that he was hallucinating. It couldn't be, but it was. Another of his kind was storming down the hallway. Ray knocked on the window. There was no doubt now. Tas stared back at him with a look that was half rage and half wonder.

"Tas! I thought you were dead."

Ray's throat closed up and his breath came in short gasps. His brother was alive! Tas said something, but the room must have been soundproof. Ray could hear nothing.

"I can't hear you. It's- You have to push the button."

Tas didn't push the button. He turned his fist to stone and smashed the door lock. It swung open easily.

Ray opened his arms wide to embrace his brother. Instead, he was treated to a punch in the face. It wasn't a stone punch, though, which might have done serious damage. No, it was just designed to knock him on his ass.

"Not yet. I'm pissed at you, and I'm busy. We'll deal with this later." Tas stormed off, leaving Ray sitting there on his ass, stunned.

"I'll find you on the ship," Ray said, finding a few words.

'Don't fucking die before then," Tas yelled. "I haven't beat the shit out of you yet."

Ray just laughed and stood up. He was pretty sure that Tas's line of destruction would be easy enough to follow to the way out. He found the elevator but rather than take the actual lift, he just climbed the shaft. With a few flutters of his wings, he made a speedy ascent and soon emerged from the top, where Tas has obviously stone punched the gate to open it.

Half of him wanted to follow Tas and get the story of how he'd survived and where he'd been for the past eighty years. The other half was desperate to get back to Jesse, to make sure that Pablo still didn't have his hands on her. He stormed out of the entrance to the base, expecting some sort of resistance. All he saw was a peaceful farm, displaying a brilliant fall picture of golden and red leaved trees.

First, he had to find out where exactly he was. Then find a phone to call. Maybe she could find a way to meet him. An engine revved and a large black SUV with tinted windows came barreling down the road. He reached to his belt where he kept his perception filter. A few seconds later and he would appear to be a middle aged man wearing a pair of jeans and a large wing collar shirt. Sure, it was a little dated, but it might pass muster better than gray winged monster.

The vehicle pulled up beside him and Ray braced himself for

a fight. There was no telling if the driver or passengers were going to come out shooting, and despite tough skin, Ray was not actually bulletproof.

"Yo. Need a lift?" As the window cracked down, Ray clearly saw Tommy in the driver's seat. He was grinning from ear to ear.

Not in the mood to look two gift horses in the mouth in one day, Ray circled around and opened the passenger side door. Jesse poured out and into his arms. He kissed her soundly until Tommy cleared his throat.

"Your friend, eh?" Tommy said. "Maybe here's not the best place for a long reunion?" He was right. Ray put Jesse back into the front seat and climbed into the back seat.

"Glad to see you too, but how did you get here?" Ray asked as Tommy took off down the road.

"I'm a full service lawyer, don't you know?"

"He called up Margaret to get Pablo. She's going to 'lose' his paperwork." Ray sighed. He hadn't meant for Tommy to get involved. He was a recent father of twins, and if Pablo ever got out, the Rose Syndicate could choose to go after him too. The more connections he had, the more they had to use against him.

"I mean, we were just sitting there, staring at the farm," Tommy said, "hoping to see someone coming or going. Think of rescue plan, and then you come sauntering out like you own the place."

"I had help, but getting as far away as possible before Rose finds out what the hell is going on is a great plan."

There was no time to explain Tas and he did pause a moment to consider going back, but Tas seemed sure enough of himself to carry on alone. It would just seed more confusion and chance that all of them would be swept up by possible reinforcements.

"Thankfully, Pablo was too lazy to drive himself very far. And he was too cheap to hire a helicopter big enough for his entire entourage," Jesse said. "You okay, though?"

"I was going to ask you the same question. And Luis? Did he make it?"

"Luis is fine. Pablo lied. Stole his phone. Luis is hanging at his cousin's for a few weeks until the heat blows over, just in case. But Tommy assures me that Pablo is going to be stuck in jail for a long time."

Relief filled Ray and he took a deep breath. Not that he didn't trust Margaret, but he'd be glad when he and Jesse were safely a galaxy or two away from the Rose Syndicate and their evil henchmen.

Tommy pulled the car into a lot with a helicopter parked. "I might have implied that I was still considering pressing charges on accomplice to attempted murder, so he's going to ferry you to the airfield. There'll be a chartered plane there ready to fly you to wherever you want to go. I'm gonna go the slow way. Rent a hotel room for the night, get a blissful night of sleep and then drive back in the morning."

Jesse reached over and hugged Tommy. "Thank you. And I really kinda wish I'd found you earlier. I think you'd be an awesome cousin."

"And you would have been a great babysitter!" Tommy grinned as he let go of the hug. "Go on, both of you."

Ray got out of the car and he and Jesse approached the helicopter. Despite having enough money to hire one, Ray had never actually flown in a helicopter. He supposed he didn't trust such a flimsy craft when he could depend on his own wings. Despite his misgivings, he slipped in beside Jesse, resisting the urge to pull her onto his lap and kiss her silly. There would be time for that. For now, just holding her hand was going to have to do.

"Holy cow," Jesse said as she stepped aboard. "This is so much better than flying commercial."

"It's expensive. I don't do it that often," Ray said as he settled into one of the seats.

"At least I can cross another thing off my bucket list." Jesse said as she sat down across from him and stroked the leather of the armrests like she was caressing a puppy.

"Please tell me you don't have parachuting on that list," Ray said.

"God, no. Why would I want to jump out of a perfectly good airplane? Besides, I think falling off a roof has spoiled me for wanting to fall." He'd elected not to pop for a flight attendant. It was just a pilot and a copilot and the two of them aboard. Privacy was always a first concern.

"No, I wasn't talking about that. I was talking about flying in a helicopter and then a private jet. Plus, you know, mile high club?" She wiggled her eyebrows at him. "Also, going to Canada. I've never been to Canada."

"It's cold."

"You've been there?"

"I have. When we first came over, I considered moving Olivia and Midge to Canada. After all, it was a part of the commonwealth, and I thought it would be closer to living at home."

"Why didn't you move there?"

"It's cold."

"Really?"

"Plus, I got a good deal on a couple of buildings in New York, and Olivia was absolutely enchanted with the city. Big, loud and alive at all hours, like London, but with no bombs falling from the skies. She used to sit outside and stare up at the skies, even when it got too light out to really see any of the stars.

I suggested several times that we go move to the country, but she wouldn't have any of it."

Despite Jesse's insistence that she actually wanted to join the mile high club, once the plane reached altitude and Ray showed her how to completely recline her seat, Jesse fell asleep.

Since he'd spent a good portion of the last few days in stone sleep, Ray felt no need to recharge. He had to draw up a list, delineating most of his holdings and what he wanted to go where. Ray thought it was safe to leave one building to Luis and the other to Giles. The bulk of his cash reserves would simply go to Tommy and his sister. They were the only family left, and Ray could trust Tommy to give a portion away to a list of nonprofits. He was a pragmatist, so it wouldn't trigger until he'd been "lost" in the Canadian wilderness for thirty days. That way, it would cover any accidents or issues, in case the sigil was malfunctioning and there really wasn't a ride home. It wasn't good to give away your fortune just when you needed back.

He'd selected to fly into Fort McMurray International Airport. They were large enough to take big jets, but there wasn't any Canadian Border Patrol presence there. He was flying without a passport, and at least Jesse had the presence of mind to grab hers. For the most part, a few dollars extra for the pilot and all those sorts of problems just disappeared. Fort McMurray was large enough to get lost in, but small enough to stay out of trouble.

From there, they would take a smaller chartered plane to Tungsten, which from all accounts. was a ghost town on the edge of the end of the world. At one point it had been a thriving mine, but it had been shut down for a few years and all the houses and buildings had been closed and left to rot. It was a great place wait for the few days to pass without any more interference from Rose Syndicate.

Ray finished his plans, and sat back with a satisfied sigh. He loved that he could just watch Jesse sleep for a long while. He smiled and relaxed until the plane began its descent.

He woke Jesse and they exited from the jet into a waiting limo.

"You were right. It is cold," Jesse said as she slid across the seats. Ray opened the mini bar for her inspection and laughed as she ogled the contents inside. Tommy must have been one smooth talker, because no one even tried to look at their passports or question them about their intentions. The limo took them on a twenty minute drive and pulled up in front of a quaint bed and breakfast that made Jesse's eyes light up. With such a reaction to a cozy human establishment, he couldn't wait to see how she'd react to a Durassian ship with all its technology.

"Why don't you go check us in?" Ray said. Jesse actually winked at him and headed off into the lobby. If the limo driver thought it was odd that they had no luggage, he said nothing. Just nodded and left without another word. Jesse bounded out a minute or two later, clapping her hands under her armpits to ward off the cold.

"We've got the executive suite, and well, I think it's better than the honeymoon suite because it has a private entrance, and a spa tub. I mean, it probably won't be as good as your rain shower, but..."

Ray felt himself harden with the memory of the shower where he nearly mated with her. This time, he would take her and the very thought of it made him impatient to get inside. Jesse seemed to share the same thought as she grabbed his hand and took him around the side of the building. She put the key in the door and opened it with a grand gesture.

"See, it's even got a king sized bed. Why this is the executive suite and not the honeymoon suite is beyond me, because if I got married I'd want to spend that night here with that tub."

"Jesse, mating on my world is more than marriage," he told her seriously.

"How can it be more than marriage?"

"Because there is no divorce. You will be mine forever."

"Oh? And what about my 'you will be mine forever', buddy? Because I won't tolerate any, you know, monkey business or multiple wives et cetera, et cetera, et cetera."

Ray shut her up with a kiss that she heartily returned. "Sweetheart," he said when he broke off the kiss. "Since I met you, there has only been you. There will only be you. I just want to make it clear that there's no going back, from this point on. If you want to change your mind, I'll understand. I'll rewrite my instructions to Tommy and you'll be set for life."

His heart ached to give her this chance, but he knew he'd regret it if he didn't and she tried to change her mind later on.

"Ray. Bite me."

JESSE

"That's not quite how it works," Ray said. The smile on his face told her that she'd amused him yet again.

"Well, then how does it work? Do I need to get naked?"

"Yes." The amusement in his voice was slipping into a more gravelly aroused. That could definitely work.

"Do you need to get naked?"

"Generally." Yes, he was definitely pressing out the front of his shorts now. Jesse suddenly wished she had something more romantic to change into. She'd been wearing the same second-hand dress since they'd left New York City and she hadn't even been able to grab a change of underwear. Ray didn't seem to care as his hands explored her legs, inching the hem of the dress up.

"I think that if we have that giganto tub, we'd better actually put it to good use. Do you have bathtubs in space?"

He let out a long laugh with that remark and Jesse shimmied out of his embrace to turn the tap on. She turned her back to him.

"Unzip me, please." He stopped laughing and stepped up to help her with the zipper.

"We don't have bathtubs per say, but we do have hot springs on Duras. I'm sure I can build you something that would meet your needs."

"Oh, and do you have the need to watch me bounce around in a bikini like Bunny?"

"Only if I can bounce you around on my cock." Ray unhooked her bra too, sliding the straps down off her shoulder with the dress. A few more light tugs and he had the dress pooling around her ankles as she she stood there in only her panties.

"I suppose something could be arranged." His hands cupped her breasts possessively before beginning to tweak her nipples into hard little points. She rubbed her ass against the bulge in his pants. She wanted to feel it inside her and soon. "I think we can test the water now."

"Not yet. It's not anywhere near full yet."

"Well, neither am I," Jesse said.

Ray stripped her panties down and for a moment, she thought he was going to push her down and enter her right there, his whole monster cock deep inside her, but Ray had other plans. He set her ass on the edge of the tub, spread her legs and knelt in front of her. He buried his tongue in her pussy and began to give her a tongue lashing that had her moaning from nearly the first moment.

She felt herself near the crest and couldn't stop herself from screaming. Ray took that as a sign and quickly flipped her onto his lap, surrounded her with his wings and sunk her down onto his waiting shaft. She pulsed around him and he growled, wrapping his arms around her hips to grind himself to his pleasure. Her breath caught and Ray pulled her forward, sinking his fangs into the fleshy part between her neck and her shoulders as his cock spasmed and released his seed inside her.

It started as a burning, then tingling warm and cool, it ran down her body, pulsing along with her heartbeat. When it reached her pussy, she exploded again, in a spiraling blaze of ecstasy that left her limp and breathless. Ray released her shoulder. He stood and dropped into the bathtub. He was still towering inside her.

"You're still hard," she said.

"Side effect of the mating. I'll probably be hard for another twelve hours or so."

"Oh really?" she asked with a raised eye. He laughed.

"I would have thought you'd be a bit worn out by now. I've been told mating can take a lot out of females, especially for women of other species."

Jesse giggled. She loved the feel of the warm water surrounding them while she was still mounted on his cock. "Oh, it took a lot out of me, but for some reason, I think I can handle a lot more. So, how do I taste?"

"Depends. To which taste are you referring? Your hot pussy or your hot blood? I will be honest. I much prefer the taste of your clit under my tongue."

Jesse swiveled her hips, rocking him just slightly out and back in. He let out a little catch breath.

"What? Are you sensitive?"

"Very."

"Good." Jesse leaned back until her hair was under the surface of the water. She came back up and reached for the bottle on the ledge. "Here. Wash my hair."

Ray pooled some of the shampoo in his palm and began to gently rub it into her hair. Not satisfied with just sudsing up her hair, Ray's hands moved lower, covering her breasts with a fine layer of bubbles, paying close attention to the tips. Of course she had to have super clean nipples.

"You're slippery," he said. Ray slid his hands up and down her sides to illustrate.

"I think you'll be able to manage if you want to."

"Oh, I want to." He reached forward, under her butt and lifted her nearly off his cock before giving her the full length. She was still so sensitive that it sent off sparks that nearly had her cumming again.

Ray sensed it and gave her even more friction. The water splashed in waves against the side of the tub as he worked her quickly to her pleasure and over the top.

"Ray!" Jesse tried to cling to him, but he decided at that moment it was time to rinse her hair. He leaned her back until her head was nearly under the water. The change in angle sent her into another wave of pleasure.

Another couple of dips and he pulled her back up.

"There. All done." He laughed as she clung to him, speechless. With a grace that Jesse would never have been able to manage, Ray got them out of the bathtub and then toweled her off. He put her on the bed before using the towel on himself, though it was clear he was just going to let his wings drip dry after a general shake.

He crouched down beside the bed, his cock still protruding obscenely, putting his arms up on the bed and just smiled at her.

"So what do we do now?" Jesse asked. She tried to stifle a yawn, but being pounded by a huge cock had taken a lot out of her.

"We wait. I don't know what changes may affect you, and I'd rather take it easy until we know for sure."

"I don't feel any different." She was a little sore, but that probably had nothing to do with his bite, and everything to do with how vigorously she had just been riding him.

"It may take a while. DNA doesn't always get rewritten in a day."

"That sounds a little ominous."

"I warned you."

"I know. But you could sugar coat it just a little."

"I'll find you just as pretty if you sprout horns."

"I'm not sure that helps."

Ray laughed. "Go to sleep. I'll be right beside you." With that, Ray's features froze and he turned to stone. It was a sight she hadn't seen too often, and it was miraculous all the same. Jesse wondered if come the morning, she'd be able to do the same.

FRELINRAY

Ray was worried, but he was not about to explain that to Jesse. Something should have happened by now, but Jesse hadn't changed at all. She'd had no reaction to the mating exchange. She was the same fragile, peppy artist that he had fallen in love with.

She wouldn't last a day on Duras. What the fuck had he done? Ray had a duty to return, no matter the cost to his own self. But if Jesse didn't change, he couldn't see how he was supposed to take her with him.

It had been over a day and they'd happily gone out shopping around Fort McMurray, buying a parka and other cold weather gear for her. Now that he had the ability to change into any form he wanted to, Ray had set his perception filter to a rather ordinary looking man closer to Jesse's age. Now, they were Mr. and Mrs. Lark, newlyweds with some cash to burn. It was nice to be able to wander around town, holding hands, window shopping like any two humans could. This is what Jesse deserved, not being thrown off some roof or shot at by fat pastel sociopaths.

It was still not too late to settle down somewhere, out of the way on the edge of the civilized world and be able to live in relative peace away from the Syndicate. Ray didn't have to join his brothers back on Duras. They could just take him for one of the dead, one of those that hadn't survived the thousand year wait.

But Tas was alive. Tas would know. He couldn't abandon his brother twice in one lifetime.

"What's up?" Jesse said as they were walking back to their bed and breakfast from dinner.

"Nothing."

"Oh, we aren't going to play that game, Spaceboy."

Ray rolled his eyes. In no way or form was he a boy.

"Tell me," she insisted.

"We don't have to go."

"You mean you dragged me all the way to fricken' Canada and the cold just to get cold feet?"

"You have yet to change and Duras is an unforgiving world."

"You're afraid to take me," she said, quietly. "You've been waiting all this time, and I'm the one holding you back."

Ray was silent. He couldn't quite put into words what he was feeling.

"I mean, it's alright if you want to go alone," Jesse said. "I'll understand. I'm defective."

Ray stopped and turned her toward him. To hell who could see, he folded his wings around her.

"You are my mate. We are bonded and I would give up all my years for you. We either stay together, or go together. I will not part from you."

Ray claimed her mouth in a kiss and she met him passionately. It was definitely time to get back to the bed and breakfast before someone noticed something protruding from his front side. He was half tempted to fly her the short walk, but instead, he grasped her hand and the pair practically ran toward their suite.

She was out of breath when he closed the door behind him, but that was not going to slow Ray down. He had the need to possess his mate, to taste her and remind himself of her strength. He chose to dwell too often on her human frailties, the body that could easily be broken and the bones snapped. He often forgot that her spirit was what drew him in, the one that let her roll with the punches and be ready to accept all problems and solutions with ease.

Ray made quick work of his shorts, and was even getting quicker at disrobing Jesse. She still laughed as his hands tangled on her bra, but he wasn't laughing, especially because she had put her hands on his cock. How the hell was he already so close to covering her with ropes of his cum? That would not do at all.

Once he'd gotten her naked, Ray pushed her back onto the bed and spread her legs. He dove between them and she let out a squeal as his tongue met her flesh. He loved the taste of her. He could spend an hour with her legs clamped around his head, feeling her hands grasping at his horns, at his hair, anything for a purchase that gave her satisfaction. Her hips bucked and he held them steady as he pushed the tip of his tail inside her and continued flicking her tender button with his tongue. He felt her spasm again and again around his tail and soon that was not enough. His neglected member had a demand of its own. He withdrew his tail.

Ray picked her up and turned her toward so that her knees were on the bed.

"Are you going to fuck my ass with your tail again?" Jesse asked. Ray thought that would have been clear the way that he was rubbing it against her pussy lips for a little extra lubrication.

"That was my plan," he said as he pushed inside her. The tender tip of his tail squeezed inside of her brought him one step closer to cumming, but it was an exquisite pleasure that he would not deny himself.

"Good, I was hoping you weren't going to make me beg."

"You can beg for my cock if you want," Ray said as he positioned himself at her entrance.

"As if you could resist my hot wet hole after all the work you just put in to making it so."

Ray laughed. "You're right." Ray guided just the head of his cock in, loving how she felt extra tight with the pressure of his tail inside her. His hands held her hips steady as she pressed against him, trying to get more of his shaft. "But I'll let you in on a little secret, sweetheart. You've got me so close I could just cum right here. I don't need any more friction."

"That's not fair," Jesse said wiggling against him, trying to get him to move inside her again. He held still, delighting in the feel of her squirming for his cock beneath him.

"Ray!"

"Yes?"

She sighed dramatically. He couldn't see but she was probably rolling her eyes. "Oh please Spaceboy, fuck me hard. Give me that tail in my ass and that cock in my pussy and ram me so hard you come out of my mouth."

Ray quickly thrust fully into her. "Like that?"

"Oh God, like that."

He began to earnestly fuck her ass with his tail.

"And like that?"

"Fuck yes."

Ray was beyond banter at that point, and so was Jesse as he settled into a demanding rhythm that had her moaning and screaming profanities in short order. Finally, the pleasure of it was too much. He buried himself deep and with his own moan, emptied himself inside her. He tried to squash the satisfaction that now she was his mate, there was a chance that his seed would take root and grow his child within her. He had watched many of his friends become fathers, grow old. There had been a slight jealousy. He'd been a father of a sort to Olivia and Midge, but he had to watch them get old and die while he still remained in his prime. It was an ache he yearned to fill with a child of his own.

Ray laid Jesse on the bed and looked over her naked and love spent body. She smiled back at him in a contentment that suggested she would probably be ready for more in another hour or so. She pressed her lips together in a smile that said she found something amusing. Ray raised a questioning eyebrow. Jesse giggled.

"If I get a tail, can I put it up your ass?"

"If you get a tail, you can put it anywhere you want."

JESSE

Tungsten was about as eerie as a town could get. It was like someone had taken a town and just left it to rot, not caring about the buildings, or the roads. Maybe Jesse had watched too many apocalyptic zombie shows. She practically expected to see a zombie wandering into view any moment now.

The pilot was just a little worried about leaving them there. He had them pegged as city slickers that wanted an adventure of a lifetime and were in way over their heads.

"I don't think you understand how cold it's gonna get tonight," he said as he unpacked their pitiful looking duffel bag of supplies.

Jesse had stopped for a parka and cold weather gear, but Ray had no need the defend against the cold. Apparently stone was not affected by the freezing weather. They only had to last a few days, and Ray was sure they could find shelter and more supplies in the buildings left by the mine.

"I know it's a cool ghost town, but getting someone to fly back here isn't going to be as easy as you think. You got a sat phone?"

"Yes," Jesse lied. She'd left her phone with Tommy in Pennsylvania. There was no use in carrying it to space, unless she wanted to play games on her phone, and then she imagined she'd have a hard time finding an appropriate charger for it. "Don't worry about us. We're more experienced than you think. He's a very good climber."

"Why the hell isn't he even wearing a jacket?" the pilot grumbled.

Jesse shrugged, knowing that Ray hadn't wanted to program in a jacket just for a short encounter with the pilot.

Despite his misgivings, the pilot gave her his phone number and left, shaking his head.

Ray told her to stay put while he scouted the town. She wanted to object, but he literally flew off. Jesse had to admit that he looked majestic finally able to spread his wings in the open air.

Jesse stamped her feet and rubbed her hands. She'd handled a winter in New York but it was nothing compared to this. She didn't think she could put on enough layers to keep warm. Jesse decided that waiting still in one place was for suckers. She grabbed the heavy duffel's strap and slung it over her shoulder. With a bit of a wobble, she walked toward the first cluster of buildings.

The cold had killed off much of the plant life, but it had apparently not stopped it from overtaking the roads in the summer. There were no sidewalks but the houses and the street were clear enough as she headed down a street.

She'd gone about three houses down when she noticed that her toes were no longer cold. In fact, they felt like they were burning. The flames were licking up her calves and getting higher. Her knees too now felt like they should be steaming. There was no pain, just an over warmth that made her want to peel her clothes off and take a run in the nippy air in just her skivvies.

Jesse knew there was no one there. There couldn't be anyone there, but modesty at least prevented her from taking off her pants. Her coat though, that could come off. She swung off the duffel and unbuttoned her parka. The heat had reached her hips now, and it was still going upward. She pulled off her sweater and unbuttoned the top few buttons on her blouse. What was this? Was this a hot flash? Was she going through some sort of early menopause?

She felt the heat climb through her body and when it reached her teeth, her eyes, she felt like the were going to explode. She clenched her eyes closed hard and when she opened them again, the world was different. Jesse could see a blazing new set of colors. They defied description and the whole thing was too overwhelming. She bent over double and collapsed onto her knees.

She must have screamed because the next moment, she felt Ray's arms around her, lifting her into the air. He carried her into the town and landed, bringing her into a room that smelled like burnt hair. It was the smell of a power generator cranking through a system that hadn't been turned on in over a year.

Ray put her down on some sort of couch and began to bundle her with blankets but she didn't need the heat. She needed the world to become less brilliant.

"I'm hot, Ray," she said, blindly shoving at the blankets he'd mounded on her.

"You shouldn't be. You were standing out in freezing weather without your coat. Are you sick?"

"This doesn't feel like sick, this feels like, whoah, I'm trippin' balls and there's swirly colors and lights everywhere."

Ray lowered the lights and Jesse opened her eyes. She could see everything, every little detail in near complete dark.

"Is this what you see in the dark? It's like I'm a cat with night vision."

"How many fingers am I holding up?" Ray said from a few

feet away. In the dim light, she shouldn't have been able to see anything.

"Three. I can see your fingers. Is that my new super power? Immunity to cold and night vision?"

"Like I said, it's different for everyone. I just didn't expect it to take so long to kick in."

There was relief in his voice though, as if he was talking with a child whose tooth had finally fallen out on its own. She was relieved, but she kept checking all of her extremities to see if she'd grown any new parts. So far, nothing had sprouted from anywhere.

With the lights dimmed, the world was not such a spectacle and Jesse could actually spend time wandering around, looking at objects with new found appreciation.

The need to peel off her clothes dissipated, and the burning slowly settled and weaned away. She was not hot, but she certainly wasn't cold. There was little to do but sit and wait to see if any other changes were on the way.

"Will I get fangs? Or wings? Or a stony exterior. Or is this it?"

"Sweetheart, I told you, I don't know, but if this was it, I think we'll be in the clear."

"Will you still love me if I get fangs?"

"Only if you bite me with them occasionally."

"I can do that." Jesse stood up and wandered around the room.

"It's a bed and breakfast," he said, answering her unvoiced question. "There are a couple of rooms that are just completely ready for a night, and some gas left in the generator. I think there's enough gas to run for the next few days, especially if we don't have to crank up the heat.

"Oh, so you're suggesting that I should take off all my clothes and cuddle body heat style?"

"My body doesn't give off as much heat as yours does, so I'm not sure that's actually going to work."

Jesse sighed. "I was hinting that we, you know, do a closer examination?"

Ray tilted her head up to look at her face. "I think you've got a set of Durassian eyes."

"And my mother's nose but the rest belongs to you." Jesse reached for his shorts.

"Sweetheart-"

"I want to see that Durassian cock with my new Durassian eyes."

She didn't give him much of a chance to object before letting it loose from its material.

"Right," Ray said. "But it's probably good to look but not tou-"

Jesse gave the tip a lick, then ran her tongue down the ridges of his shaft. She circled one of the bumps at the base of his cock and then another. She loved how it grew and hardened against her cheek.

Ray tried again. "You might be in a delicate stage right now. It's probably best not to- Oh."

Jesse trailed back to his head and took it entirely into her mouth, swirling her tongue as she went. She loved the taste of him, salty and sweet like some kind of expensive salted caramel. His taste seemed even more pronounced than the last time she'd taken his cock in her mouth. She worked his cock, ruthlessly, mercilessly and Ray couldn't stop himself from tangling his hands in her hair.

"Jesse!" It was a warning, but Jesse knew it was coming, wanted him to shout out and fill her mouth with his load. Jesse felt his cock pulse and tighten and then she had it, spraying into her mouth, thick and satisfying. When she'd swallowed it all, she looked up at Ray and he gathered her up into his arms.

She settled on his knee with her arms wrapped around his neck.

"Did I ever tell you that you taste like an expensive cupcake?"

"That's not very sexy," Ray said.

"On the contrary. I find cupcakes very sexy."

⚜

"Happy Halloween!" Ray called out to Jesse. She sat up straight and blinked hard.

"Sorry. It's my favorite Earth holiday, and I guess I get a little excited." Ray smiled at her and held out his hand. Jesse opened hers and he dropped a chocolate in her hand.

"Trick or treat."

Jesse popped the chocolate in her mouth, savoring the flavor. Ray swooped in for a kiss, and when he lifted his head, Jesse realized the chocolate was no longer in her mouth.

"Trick," Ray said. He held up another chocolate and put it between his teeth.

"You are a very bad boy," Jesse said as she reached up for another kiss. It was hot and chocolaty all in one.

"I've been waiting a long time for something like this. To be close to someone, and for it to be so easy," he mused.

She smiled and finished her hard earned chocolate.

"So I think it's best we try to do this in stages. I take a bag, and then you, up in stages."

"And what if they come while I'm on the side of the mountain and you're flying around?"

"I don't anticipate they'll pick us up before noon. We'll be high enough by then."

A short time later and they were making their way up the mountain. The air was thinner, Jesse could feel that in her lungs, but the cold hadn't bothered her yet. This whole immune-tofrostbite thing was actually turning out to be a pretty good super power. Ray had just left their current ledge to take the bag even higher. They were well above the tree line and the ledges were getting smaller and smaller. The one he left her on was about ten feet across, and she didn't even try to go near the edge. Falling off a roof was enough of heights for the year.

There was a noise of something just out of view. It was scrambling up the cliff side below her. At first, Jesse thought it was a bird or some other small animal. Then, a shaggy head appeared over the face of the head. It was a blond mop of hair and a pair of crystal blue eyes. The man clawed his way up the ledge and Jesse backed up against the mountain. A scraggly beard appeared and then with a huff, he completed a roll onto the safety of the ledge. He was wearing a fur parka and looked like one of those mountain men of old, a grand viking who would probably be nearly seven feet when standing. He was young though, no more than twenty.

"You got any beef jerky? I am starving," he said. Jesse just stared at him. "Hell, I'd take a power bar if you'd got it. Anything? English. French? Ruski?"

Jesse dug into her bag and pulled out the bag of potato chips she'd been saving for a rainy day. Who knew if they had potatoes in space?

"Oh. My. God. You are such a life saver." He took the bag of chips and opened it without getting up. He crunched them up in the bag and poured them directly into his mouth. "Oh, the delishush delishush sal!"

For such a large, disheveled man, he seemed quite harmless.

"What are you doing here?" Jesse asked as soon as he'd cleared his mouth.

"I'm climbing a mountain! Why am I climbing a mountain, you ask? That was going to be your next question, wasn't it?"

"Yeah."

"I'm not climbing it because it's there, if that's what you

think. I'm climbing it because… hell if I know. I was told to. It's a long story and I'm not exactly sure why, but when you are given warnings of dire consequences of not climbing a mountain in the middle of fucking nowhere Canada that's cold as fuck, you go climb the fucking mountain!"

She wasn't sure who he was shouting at. Jesse was pretty sure it wasn't her, but some unseen or remembered person from his past.

"The real question is, why are you climbing the mountain? And why aren't you cold?" he asked her.

He sat up and gave her a once over, his eyes examining her from head to foot.

"That is also a long story."

"It doesn't appear either one of us is going anywhere," he said. "I need a break. Mountain climbing is surprisingly hard work, especially without much gear." He wiggled his eyebrows and got comfortable on the ledge.

"There's not guaranteeing you're going to believe a word of it," she warned.

"Those are the best kinds of stories. I've met all sorts of people in my day, and I find the most interesting ones are just one hair short of crazy."

"I started dating an alien, and he's going to take me back to his mother ship. Not the original one he came on, because that crashed. And I'm not cold because he's bit me, you know, like a vampire, and I've got some of his alien DNA rattling around in my cells now."

"Ah."

"You see, crazy."

"Not really. Is your boyfriend named Rocky?"

Jesse paused and squinted at him. He didn't look like a gargoyle, but it was possible he had a device like Ray did that altered his appearance. Ray had said it worked best on individuals that already merged with their surroundings. What else would she expect to see up here on the mountain than an actual mountain man?

Jesse reached over and touched his forehead. He froze and let her run her hand up under his hood and into his hair. She felt the little nubbin of a horn, but his image didn't waver like it had with Ray. He still remained the white blond viking.

"Yeah, I bet so. Because honestly, why else would anyone be climbing this mountain on Halloween?" he said as she pulled back.

"But you're not-"

"Khargal? Nah, I'm only half. My mom was a full-blooded American and I was the apple of her eye, but she was always cold. Loved her sweaters."

"Ray said that it affects every person differently, the uh-transfer. What about your father?"

"Oh, he's shattered into a couple of thousand pieces. There are some nasty people out there, you know?"

"I know. There was this guy back in New York that tried to throw me off a roof! Then he tried to shoot me."

"He dead yet?"

"No. Pablo was made a guest of the federal prison system, and I was promised that his paperwork would get lost."

"Pablo? He got a last name?"

"No. He's like Madonna. Or Cher. He has a penchant for pastel suits and was shot in the neck by his wife, but unfortunately, it didn't kill him. Then he killed his wife, or at least said he did. I didn't independently verify that information. Mainly because he got homicidal on me like thirty seconds later, so I just assumed he was telling the truth."

"And your guy didn't kill him?"

"No. He offered, but I suppose I'm more of a pacifist at heart. I didn't have the heart to ask him to murder a murderer, even if he deserved it."

"Huh."

"Huh?"

"Huh." The golden grizzly laid back down and appeared to be deep in thought. "So why are we climbing this mountain, anyway?"

"Because the sigil told us that this was the pick up location?"

"Sigil?"

"The medalliony thingy?"

"The one with the blinky light in the middle?"

"Yeah."

"Ha. I've been calling it a thing-a-ma-gig. Told I have to get up to the top of the mountain by Halloween or… else."

"Else?"

"It'll explode. Like a nuclear bomb."

Ray chose that moment to swoop in, flying fast and landed on the chest of the half man, half alien.

"Whoah, dude!"

Jesse wasn't sure who was more surprised, Ray or the man. They both looked at her with some sort of wonder.

"I didn't mean for it to come out like that," she explained, "but… but- that guy is here for the same reason we are."

Ray gave him a good look over. Then he actually smelled him, like a large sniff.

"This guy has a name," said the guy. "Erlend. And your guy is very heavy."

"You are not full Khargal," Ray said, but to his credit, he slid to the side, removing most of his weight from Erlend's chest.

"Nope. Half and half. You know, like the stuff they put in coffee. All good and perfectly harmless."

"Most people that claim to be totally harmless are quite dangerous," Ray replied.

"Yeah, I get that, I swear. Your girl over there was just filling me in on the situation."

"Don't you know the situation?"

"I'm beginning to think I don't know the whole of it. I mean,

I was told to bring this thingy to the top of the mountain or it would explode." He reached inside his coat and pulled out a sigil. "A big boom, a couple of city blocks at least."

Ray snickered.

"What?"

"You're an idiot to fall for that load of crap," Ray said, standing up.

Erlend just lay there.

"You mean I have been climbing and starving up on this mountain for a grand load of crap?"

"The sigil isn't going to explode. Doesn't even have the capability to. It'll fizzle if they decide to activate the auto destruct, but that would be less dangerous than a toaster catching on fire."

"A toaster on fire? You sure? I mean, maybe my source is more knowledgeable than yours."

"I've rebuilt them from scratch. They don't go boom. It's impossible."

"Then... why did he-"

"It's our ride home," Ray said.

"We're gonna get sucked up into a spaceship and go travel the universe," Jesse added.

Erlend was quiet. He sat up and looked at the pair.

"I think we've got a few more thousand feet to go," Ray said. "I found a good place to wait, I think. It should be shielded from the wind." He looked at Erlend.

"I can take her and then come back for you," he told him.

"Aren't I a little big for that?"

"I'm not going to leave a Khargal on the side of a mountain so close to getting home."

Erlend nodded and shrugged. "It's up to you. Now that I know I'm not carrying a bomb, well, there's no rush."

Ray rolled his eyes and scooped up Jesse into his arms. With a few broad strokes of his wings, he flew up, spiraling against the air currents, getting higher and higher with each powered surge. Jesse did not want to look down. Even the trees looked tiny from up here. A large bird flapped below them.

"Wait, is that another gargoyle?" Jesse asked.

"Might be," Ray said. He didn't look. He had his eyes glued to a large outcrop just above them. He landed on it and settled Jesse there. There was a hollow place there for them to sit and wait.

"Are you sure it's high enough?"

"It should be. Honestly, I think anything above the tree line should be fine, but I don't want to take any chances," Ray said.

"So Erlend might be fine where he is?"

"Possibly. You have a problem with Erlend?" Ray asked.

"You're already tired as it is. He's right. He's kinda big. I'd rather you didn't plummet to your death right before we leave."

Ray kissed her. "I'll be careful, but just in case," he said, pulling the sigil out of his shorts. "You hold on to this, because if something happens to me, this is probably the only way you're getting off this mountain alive."

"But what if they transport me without you by accident?"

"Sweetheart, you just tell them to wait and come for me. Scream bloody murder. I'm sure someone will listen."

"Right," Jesse said half sarcastically, but Ray just smiled and took a dive off the edge of the cliff. She was once again left alone to face the upcoming alien beam out by herself.

FRELINRAY

It was unnerving, seeing the large man, the halfling, so close to his unprotected mate, but Ray hadn't let his first instincts color his second opinion of Erlend. He was young and stupid, but he deserved every benefit of the doubt. Ray could take him under his wing and show him the world of his father, since his own must not be able to.

Jesse was right. Ray was tired. His body begged for a stone sleep, but he was not willing to let exhaustion claim him yet. He would struggle with the large half breed until they were both on the ledge. It was the only thing he could do, penance for leaving Tas behind decades earlier. Had he known Tas was still alive, he could have returned and pulled him to safety or tried to rescue him from whatever clutches the Rose Syndicate had placed him in.

He would not, could not abandon Erlend.

Ray looked down to see that Erlend had climbed another fifty feet in his absence. He was now sitting on a small ledge, barely big enough for two Khargals. Ray fluttered down and crouched beside him. Erlend just surveyed the mountain below.

"Who is your father?"

"Faso. A bit of an old curmudgeon. Never figured out how to dial a rotary phone, nevermind a cell phone, but he was my old man."

Ray knew him well. He was small for a Khargal, quick and light on his feet, and smart as a whip.

"Your mother must have been a very large woman," Ray stated.

Erlend threw back his head and laughed. "I like you," he said. "You actually have a sense of humor."

"Where is Faso?"

"The Rose Syndicate smashed him to pieces," Erlend responded, gritting his teeth.

Ray's heart twisted a little. "I hope that you made them pay."

"I'm good at that," Erlend grinned humorlessly. "You know what I suck at? Climbing mountains. I'm a city boy. Now, I want to ask you a question. This space ship ride, is it a two way? Or a one way trip?"

Ray shrugged, but he pretty much knew the answer.

"It's my guess that after a thousand years, they're not going to just say, oops, my bad, and plop you back down on the mountain."

"That's what I was figuring. When I started this gig, I thought, hey, doing the world a favor. I wasn't thinking, oh yeah, I'm leaving on a space plane. Don't know when I'll be back again. I mean, I got a cat. How am I supposed to just abandon the poor thing?"

Ray nodded. "You don't want to go. I get it."

"No hard feelings though?"

"No. In fact," Ray said, reaching for his belt. He took off his perception filter and handed it over to Erlend. "This is a handy bit of tech. It'll keep you under cover. It only works on people, not machines and mostly from a bit further away."

"Seriously. That'll come in handy. I still have some Rose to go after. I hear there's a guy named Pablo that needs an eye kept on him."

"Two eyes, wide open, preferably," Ray told him.

"I'm sneaky. I've figured out how to keep them on their toes from a maximum distance. I guess I don't need this anymore," he said, handing Ray his sigil. Ray accepted it, nodding.

Ray surveyed the mountainside. "I can probably get you down a few thousand feet, but you'll be on your own from there."

"Nah, no need. It's only the going up that's the problem. I've got going down covered, if I don't freeze my ass off first."

Erlend threw off his coat to reveal a broad chest that was backed with a pair of small, lightweight wings that mostly folded back into his shoulder blades. Ray realized that he didn't have the muscles needed to flap the wings, he could only glide. Not very elegant, but it would get him down in a hurry.

"Good luck. Live long and prosper and all that shit, and thanks." Erlend gave a wave before extending his wings and gliding down the mountain with his coat in his arms.

Ray stood, planning to fly himself when the sigil in his hand flashed a wild light. It was coming. There was no time left to fly to Jesse. He took one last gaze at the planet that had been his home for nearly a millennium and sighed. There were things he would miss. Duras was a long ago memory. How much had his planet changed in the past thousand years? Would he be an arti-fact, like his technology was likely to be? What had spurred a rescue at this point in time? Why hadn't they come earlier?

He felt the warm tingling he'd been expecting and closed his eyes to fight back the nausea. A few seconds later, Jesse was standing nearby, puking her guts out on the polished deck of he transport pad.

"What. The. Fuck." she said between retches.

Two Khargals stood at attention in full dress uniform in front of them.

"Frelinray, Engineer, first class?" one of them asked Ray.

Ray straightened up. "Aye." The Khargal warriors looked over at Jesse, slightly less impressed.

"Your mate has a weak stomach."

"You try having your atoms scrambled for the first time," Jesse retorted. "Felon Ray?"

"Frelinray, it's my name."

"So is Ray your last name?" Ray shook his head and sighed. "Jesse, this is a conversation for another time and place."

The Khargal on the left let out a huff of disapproval. The one on the right elbowed his compatriot.

"We are not to judge. He is a war hero." He gave a nod. "We are to escort you to your quarters before meeting the captain."

Ray nodded and the pair turned crisply and walked out into the hallway. He took Jesse's hand and they followed. Ray saw very little to indicate technological innovation from the past thousand years. In fact, he recognized most of the components as things he knew how to work with and could easily maintain as an engineer. His fear of being obsolete was apparently over thought.

The light curved walls and system of honeycombed pillars were so different than what he'd gotten used to on Earth, but they were familiar in his now distant memory. He didn't have to constantly be aware of bumping his head on a doorway or clutching his wings close to his body. There were no silly backs on chairs to cramp his wing tips either.

Jesse had been quiet since his little warning, but her eyes were darting everywhere like a kid trying to catch every detail of a carnival ride.

Their escort stopped short in front of a cabin. It was the quarters of an officer or an official. Ray expected a superior to greet them and explain but instead, the guard indicated it was their cabin. Such quarters were not the generally small and tight shared space of a mated crewman, but Ray was not going to complain.

"The captain will be with you shortly." The door closed and Ray turned to Jesse. She looked at him expectantly.

"Are you okay?" she asked.

"I was about to ask you the same thing." They both let out a huff of amusement.

"Is this what you were expecting?" Jesse said, scanning the room. For a ship this size, it was a large room, with a table and chairs, a cleansing room and a lounging couch.

"No. Not at all. I've been away for a thousand years, and this is, well, nearly the same as I left it. And these quarters, they are what you'd call the red carpet treatment. A simple engineer would never merit such spacious quarters."

"He said you were a war hero. There's a war?"

"My planet is at war with the Ektop. It has consumed everything. Our entire mission was to find resources to help end the war. We crashed after a solar flare knocked us off course."

"What kind of war lasts a thousand years?"

"I don't know. I imagine the war ended years ago, and we were just not worth retrieving. I don't know what's changed." Ray went to the storage area and nearly cried when he opened the drawer to find several uniforms. He immediately shucked off his old cloth and slipped on a fresh uniform. Jesse giggled.

"Oh, my God, I've never seen you with actual clothes on."

"What do you think?"

"You can still put on a fedora." Ray smiled and stepped toward Jesse but the short ding stopped him in his tracks.

The door opened and a large Khargal stepped through the doorway. He wore the insignia of a captain and the bearing to match. The fangy smile he flashed Jesse reminded Ray of a few officers promoted beyond their skill, simply because of their predecessors' bad luck or their own family connections.

"Well met, brother," he said. "I am Captain Traver, and we are honored to be your escort home."

Ray said nothing. There was something odd about this man's cordiality.

"So how's the war?" Jesse said after a long silence.

"The war is over. We were victorious, and now we have come back to reclaim those that were fallen."

"I wasn't fallen. Our ship crashed. Where have you been for the past thousand or so years?" Ray demanded.

"Ah, this is a question many of your shipmates have been asking. There is a distortion, between here and Duras. According to Durassian time, you've only been gone for twenty years. It has taken this long for the war to end and for us to begin making amends."

"Amends?"

"Of course, you will receive a generous retirement package, and there will be opportunities for you to tell the tale of your years to the masses. Share anything you learned while surviving on a savage and primitive planet."

"Hey, that's my home you're talking about," Jesse said, testily.

'You do not even have a colony in space yet. You're just an orbital society, not worth the blink of our attention," Traver responded.

Jesse looked at Ray to back her up. He just shrugged.

"You've come a long way in the past forty years, but you are practically savages," Ray said.

"Thanks. Just, thanks," Jesse replied.

Ray wasn't going to lie, but he also wasn't going to buy the full line of bullshit this captain was feeding them.

"Why? Why have you come back to get us when you could have just as easily left us there and written us off as dead?"

The captain leaned in, as if he were whispering a secret.

"The Council has made some unpopular decisions lately. They saw this as an opportunity to-"

"It's a PR stunt," Jesse said, finally catching on.

"I do not know what this means," the captain stumbled. Ray knew exactly what it meant.

"It means that you want me to parade around Duras, singing the praises of the Council, and making them look good," Ray spat out.

"Did I mention the compensation?" The captain was looking more uncomfortable by the second.

"Really." Jesse crossed her arms over her chest. "A fricken thousand years and that's what he gets? What kind of compensation?"

"That's negotiable. I have been given a sum of credits to be divided among those who-"

"What if we want to stay?" Ray asked.

"Credits really wouldn't do you any good on such a primitive planet."

"So the sum is divided among those who wish to go home," Ray clarified. That was an even smaller number yet. "But I was not asking about the credits. If we wished to stay and live out our lives on Earth, that would not be objectionable." Jesse wasn't sure if that was a question or a statement.

"Objectionable is a hard word. Definitely not preferable, but allowable, if that's what you are asking," Traver conceded.

"Then I will discuss it with my mate, and let you know of our decision," Ray said, turning away.

The captain was not used to being given such a curt dismissal, but Ray knew that his seniority gave him a little leeway. The captain was in a tough spot, trying to both appease his bosses back on Duras and pay homage to the ones he needed to coax back to the planet for a photo shoot. He nodded to Ray and left.

"You're not seriously thinking about staying? I mean, the Rose Syndicate is still down there, I mean, if we're still near Earth," Jesse reminded him.

"Probably hiding around the back of the moon," Ray smirked.

"Do you do that often? Hide around the back of moons?"

"If the primitives have telescopes."

"Primitives. Ha."

"Jesse, I can't guarantee any kind of a life for you up here. Duras is a hard planet."

"Do we have to go to Duras? I mean, you guys have ships that travel the galaxies. Surely there's a place for us."

"This isn't West Side Story," Ray said.

"I hope not. In case you forgot, they both die in the end." Jesse wiggled her eyebrows and they both started laughing. "Ray, I made my decision a long time ago. There's very little that I'm going to miss back on Earth. Imagine the things I can see and the paintings I could create! Especially with my new eyes."

Ray didn't have the heart to tell her that Khargal art really didn't involve much canvas work. In that case though, she'd probably be unique. No. He could take her to Duras and then explore the cosmos. He had all his designs and pretty much the entire hard drive of his computer. He'd put them on a memory chip that he'd salvaged and had been wearing in his shorts since the sigil activated. He could take the credits and build a ship to travel wherever they wanted.

"All right. But I need to speak to Tas before I make a deal. I have a feeling the captain is holding out on us."

EPILOGUE

JESSE

Jesse stood on the platform feeling big as a house. The doctors had promised her that it was normal to be this size, but she swore it felt like she was carrying twins (or rocks). Maybe twin rocks. Either way, waddling all the way down to the shipyard had not been her idea of a great time. Ray had insisted on it. Their new ship was ready.

He just wasn't ready to let her inside it just yet.

"Ray, I gotta pee!" she shouted out. Several of the Khargals standing nearby let out a snicker. Ray apparently hadn't heard her because he was taking his sweet time. He'd been working on the ship nearly the entire time they'd been on Duras. It was easy to know how long that had been, considering she was nine months pregnant and ready to pop any day now.

Much to her surprise, when they'd landed and the medics had sent her through quarantine, they'd also coldly announced that the embryo inside her was viable and healthy. No congratulations or sugar coating it from Khargal docs. No, they believed that medical advice and opinions were given as straight forward and quickly as possible. When she'd asked about how far along she was, one of them looked at her like a little child and explained that conception had probably taken place just before she'd gone through the change. It was common in lesser species.

So Jesse had gotten pregnant in Canada. It was enough to make a girl cry. Or want to pee. Jesse really needed to pee. She stormed up to the door.

"Ready or not, here I come!"

She headed up the ramp and into the main cabin of the ship. The design was unique. It had similar elements to the craft that took them here, but there were definitely human influences present. She could see tall curved archways like Durassian ships, but at the edge of the columns were definite scrollwork designs that could have been ripped off of a medieval or gothic church.

"Please, I was just trying to get-" Ray came out of one of the rooms.

"Pee. Otherwise, I'm gonna let loose all over the floor of your new ship."

"Our new ship."

"Well, our baby is sitting on my bladder, so point the way, buster."

Ray guided her toward a room. She bypassed the giant bed and headed straight for the bathroom. She hiked up her dress and nearly cried when she saw the huge sunken bath and the rain shower that were practically identical to the ones she'd drawn almost a year ago. There was even a fedora angled on one edge of the bathtub.

"Took me a while to manage the autograv safeties. Didn't want you to drown if we lost gravity," Ray said. "What are you crying for? You don't like it? I can change it."

Ray rung his hands and stared around the bathroom like he was trying to figure out what to take a sledge hammer to first.

"I love it! These are happy tears. I'd hug you but I'm still peeing!" Jesse said.

Ray sighed with relief. Jesse finished emptying her bladder.

"I thought water was a scarce commodity."

"Yeah, you'll have to wait until we make a stop somewhere to fill the tanks. Everything's set up for both water and waterless cleaning," Ray said. "I'd show you the engine room next, but I think most of that would be over your head."

"Pretty much."

"This is our bedroom," Ray said, leading her back out. She'd been in such a rush to pee that she hadn't really been paying attention.

She saw the crib in the corner with a mobile of spaceships flying above it. They had agreed to keep the baby in their room for the first few months. She'd spent nearly a month gathering up the right colors and shapes to make the mobile while Ray had a made the crib.

"Now why don't I show you your room?"

"I thought this was my room?"

"This is our room. Your room," he said.

Ray took her hand and guided her to another room. She had one thing to say. It had really good light.

"I know you can't exactly have natural lighting on a ship traveling between stars, but I hope this will be sufficient. This is maximum. You can totally change it. And I had to guess at most of the supplies or make due. It's hard to find some of the pigments and the resins here. I'm sure with a few more months, I can finish it to nearly what you had at Olivia's."

He'd built her a studio on the ship. The tears started to come again. This time, he enfolded her in his arms and wings and held her while she tried to stop sniveling.

"Good tears?" Ray asked.

"I love you," Jesse stated.

"I know."

"We'll fly the stars collecting art supplies," he said after a long moment.

"That sounds ridiculous."

"You know, we could even go back to Earth. They might

have made enough progress to join the civilized world. After all, it's been over thirty years."

"Probably not."

Ray shrugged. "Probably not, but we love them anyway."

THE END

Thank you for reading

I hope you enjoyed reading about Jesse and her Raygoyle. Find out what happens to Tas and how he manages epic escapes and rescues in *Taken for Granite* by Nancey Cummings.

About halfway through writing I decided that Margaret the FBI agent needed a Khargal of her own to have an adventure with. Stay tuned for a sequel in which Erlend is going to match wits and continue his quest to wipe The Rose Syndicate off the map.

GLOSSARY

At-Ukris: aerial Duras animal. Looks like a cross between an eagle and an octopus roughly the size of a whale

Bansial: the Durassian word for sticky

Canikin: the Durassian word for lady parts

Dam: mother

Dassa: mating fluid

Duramna: stone form

Duras: Khargal home planet

Durassian: the Khargal language

Earthian: what Khargals call humans

Fa: the Durassian word for Mrs.

Grack: the Durassian expletive for fuck

Guurlk: Khargal liquor

Hondassa: Mate

Kher: Khargal term for siblings

Khargal: what gargoyles call themselves

Lar: the Durassian word for god

Macero: the Durassian expletive for hell

Maztek: Duras animal similar to an earth whale

Rose Syndicate: clandestine organization that is pursuing gargoyles and their technology

Sartek: a random predatory animal on Duras

Sigil: the device used for contacting the rescue beacon and tele-porting to the rescue ship

Sire: father

Tanem: the Durassian word for temporary companion taken before a true mate

Want more sexy Khargals? Check out all the books in the series! You don't want to miss a single one!

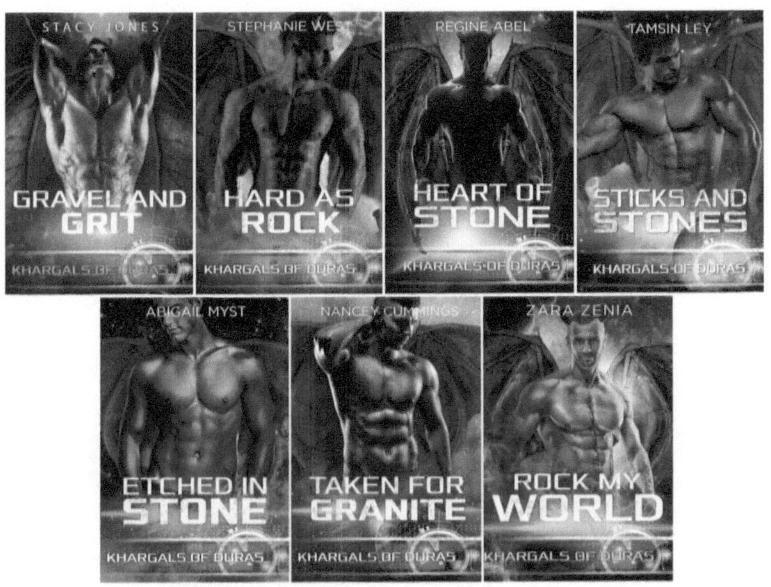

https://nanceycummings.com/khargals-of-duras/

If you liked *Etched in Stone*, check out my *Warriors of Etlon* series:

Athen

Athen doesn't want a mate. He is determined not to be the sixth brother to leave behind a widow in the war to rid the evil Suhlik from the universe. When his warriors requested a mail order bride behind his back, there is no denying his instant attraction to Odette, the Terran female. She is everything he could wish for but he is determined not to claim her for her own protection.

To Odette, a simple Earth botanist, the match to an alien is a chance for a fresh start to get away from a cheating fiance and an overbearing mother. Can she strip down Athen's defenses and win his heart before he sends her away forever?

Snowed in With the Alien Doctor

Clover is not in the market for Forever. She's a cargo captain, finally out from under a man's thumb. She's footloose and fancy free with no one to answer to but herself. She's not ready for strings Unfortunately, the handsome green alien doctor will accept nothing less.

One intoxicating sniff and Orth was hooked. Before colliding with Clover, Orth's biggest challenge was deciding which female species to specialize in. Now his nose was telling him there was no other choice but Clover. The only problem is that she's not interested in a lifetime. Can Orth win her heart and convince her that he's worth spending forever with before it's too late?

Kave

He'd found his match at last. Humility. It was an odd name, a name that Kave had repeated to himself over and over again. His DNA match was everything he had expected her to be when he requested her. Her survival skills made her worthy of Athen's clan. Too bad she'd stabbed him in the chest the moment they'd met.

Humility really managed to screw things up. When the Ministry of Alien Affairs had come knocking at her door, offering her a deal she couldn't refuse, she seized on the possibility to heal her war damaged father. Now she only had to convince her new alien husband to pull the right strings. Kave probably wasn't going to be very cooperative with her knife stuck in his chest.

Can Kave and Humility overcome their unfortunate first encounter to start and heal the family they have always wanted to have?

Zenik

A warrior duty's is sacrifice. Zenik sacrificed everything for his people - his name, his honor and even his life. He never expected to survive. Now he's been rewarded for his mission's failure with retirement and an irresistible mate, Jane. A warrior in her own right, the Terran female is his match in every way. Retirement is looking better and better. When he has the opportunity to finish his last mission and exact revenge on the male who tried to end his life, can he leave Jane?

Jane understands duty. As a soldier, she's prepared to battle alien forces for the safety of Earth. Being married off to an alien? Doesn't seem that different than fighting aliens. Her alien husband is handsome and shy. She knows he's keeping secrets but when she's in his arms, sharing passionate kisses, she doesn't care about duty or missions. He's her man.

Now he thinks he can leave her behind while he goes off on some suicide mission? He's got another thing coming.

ABOUT ABIGAIL

The Handyman is actually the first naughty story that I wrote, but it was secret until I was inspired to write Slut of Frankenstein as a contest with my friend, Nancey Cummings. There's nothing like a road trip and a bottle of wine to get the juices flowing. Once my secret was out, I couldn't get enough of writing them.

Then I discovered the world of Alpha Aliens and became a Starr Huntress. Because seriously… aliens are hot! I currently live in Philadelphia with my dog, my cats and my ever patient favorite fan. When I'm not writing, I enjoy computer games, cheesy sci-fi TV, and crafting.

Keep up with my shenanigans:
Sign up for the newsletter: http://eepurl.com/cCXDQn

Twitter https://twitter.com/AbigailMyst

Facebook https://www.facebook.com/100007815766717